I0772713

The Dead
and the Desperate

by

Dan Denton

ROADSIDE PRESS

copyright

foreword by A.S. Coomer

Dan Denton's pen sings songs of desperation, threnodies for the dead. Songs full of ugly, sure, but there's a beauty to the melody that only stems from scraping by by the sallow skin of cavity-riddled stubs of teeth through never-ending hard times. Those soul-smoldering days of ache and pain, of blisters and torn calluses, reopened wounds never given the chance to move beyond infection, and heartbreak from all sides. Buk's bluebird calls out that it really is war all the time and Denton nods with hard-earned understanding. Denton writes, "But my heart held more hurt than most men, and I'd been angry since the day I was born."

Watch the tombstone of the American Dream slowly erode in the wicked winter wind of end-stage capitalism. Watch the Rust Belt flecks flit and dance, strain your machine-deafened ears to hear their swan song carried off into the lightless night. Denton asks the dust, but the unexpected blast of life's furious sucker punch blots out any answer proffered. Everybody knows life never fights fair, it's one of the reasons the seats of the coliseum are always filled, it's why America's longest running disaster tourism reality show is COPS, it's why no one can peel their eyes from the trainwreck in front of us all.

See the lowest moment in someone's journey and gawk if you like but know no amount of money or status can protect you in the end. Just ask Siddhartha. Denton sings the Buddha's final chorus: All individual things pass away. Strive on, untiringly.

There're glimmers of hope spilling out in the heat and steam of a factory harvested heart pumping in spite of the poison coursing through its clotted veins and an environment hellbent on extracting every ounce of blood it can move. There are moments of relative bliss found in the friction of strangers, a lover's wet mouth, the susurrated static snow giving way for a classic country song to buzz out of yet another thrift store radio, the first hit from a cheap bottle, a nap stolen from the timeclock, a supervised visitation with the children. Little victories. Making these moments outshine the darkness is the battle of the dead and the desperate, of us all; Denton writes, "And I was willing to agree that 10 minutes of Heaven was better than a lifetime in purgatory." Denton reminds us "Purgatory is a rough motherfucking neighborhood to live in." Latch on to what you can.

But Denton knows these moments are fleeting. Of course they are. Besides suffering, what isn't? Denton seeks life in snatches as bright and transitory as firecrackers. Life shooting out in spurts and gurgles from a faucet nearly closed with lime and mold. Life in the last swallow from a beat-up flask. Life in the ghost-making smoke billowing from a bent spoon. Life in the prickling kiss of the needle. Little ovals of life from someone else's prescription bottle. Life from a one-night stand.

The dead and the desperate try to move beyond childhood traumas, where "the one that yells the loudest and the longest wins the argument." Where a mother makes more trips to the sanitarium for electroshock treatment than PTA and parent-teacher meetings. Later, the dead and the desperate learn "there's no reason to boast of it. Scars caused, and scars earned, are lessons, not trophies." The broken love of a son for his deeply damaged mother burned hot enough for the grown man to seek numbness, to run blindfolded out into the hawthorn patch surrounding him. Pulling off the blindfold is only part of the journey.

The dead and the desperate are often lost, but those permanently branded with the blue collar know "the factory is true north for blue collar hearts." Direction and security through the routine of the day-to-day factory life; "I just put my boots on everyday, and showed up, and tried to protect my heart from being eaten by the factory machines." The factory takes and with a miser's avarice provides a sliver to live on. They call factories "plants" because "they plant work boots on concrete. / They plant empty dreams in human hearts. / They plant blood and sweat and arthritis. / They plant broken homes in local communities and hang climate change in all our broken windows." Denton deals out the macro with his micro; The Dead and the Desperate is a self-aware autopsy of the failed American Dream. "In a barren wasteland, post Ronald Reagan America, American factories are called plants because they grow money for Wall Street farmers who don't even bother to leave black granite plaques with the names of those it's eaten alive." And it's not like the things the factories produced escape the crush of the money grinding machinations of the owners of the machines. Denton writes, "They stopped manufacturing appliances with hearts because making things with hearts cost too much, and poor factory workers in tiny apartments didn't have any money to spend on unnecessary heart. They've always had to find their own." Denton reminds us, "There's only so much blood you can mine in a poor neighborhood" and "the most generous always seem to have the least, and the ones that have the most in America? They're on the internet news headlines every day, legendary for skipping taxes and planting new and aggressive cancers all over earth."

Sometimes there is a dead man's balance on the knife's edge. A liminal period where it "didn't feel like a time of celebration, but it also wasn't a time of death. It was purgatory, and nobody much can endure the weight of the waiting." Tom Petty knew "the waiting is the hardest part." For the dead and the desperate life is a purgatorial existence ground out between the factory and the bottle, the weekly rate hotel and the backseat of a beater Chevy Cavalier, the drunk tank and child support hearings, hangovers and overtime, American life and American death.

Fast families are formed in the impossible pressure cooker factories, forged under the furious heat of the factory and the unforgiving anvil of end-stage capitalism; "we got to be pretty tight after a few months of singing the cancer dust factory blues together." These friendships lessen the burden for however long the internal flame can be protected from the howling roar of the machines. But the factory is a microcosm, much like high school and jail. There are cliques and those that lash out and bully and demean and seek dominance. Denton writes, "every factory that I've ever called home has had its own wavelength. Its own energy and local flavor, and none of them like the new guy. The new guy sticks out, and no factory has ever cared for anyone that stands out." Factories are "all tough places to survive, and they all bear their own brand of institutionalization. The factory is similar to jail in that it's likely the new guy is going to have to stand up for himself at least once, and pretty quick to fit in. If you don't, one of two things is going to happen: you're gonna get taken advantage of, or you ain't gonna make it…It gets so a man living a hard life feels like he's always in a new spot so much, that he's always got to stand up to someone to prove he's not to be taken advantage of."

A whole generation of blue-collar American men who "worked and showered and learned how to hold a baby girl in one hand, and a beer in the other." That money-making lie—the American Dream—where the worker gives "away tiny pieces of [their] dreams a factory hour at a time." Parents at the factory while their children take their first steps. "You'll stand next to machines that spit cancer dust in your eyes all day, and if you have a family, you will spend more time making memories with the cancer machine than you will with that family." Families of factory workers moving around the absences in their homes, Denton writes, "They couldn't shut down the furnaces for Santa Claus, the Easter Bunny, Labor Day parades or Thanksgiving turkeys. So whole generations of glass making families have gone their whole lives incomplete at the holidays."

The misfit cast of society's castoffs scrap and claw with broken-hearted desperate nails at what glints of love and comfort can be found and fight for some bastard sort of security in a world that makes it perfectly clear there is no security for the working class. They fight wars of insecurity with the factory, the landlord, the lover with "everything our trauma laced brains could think of as weapons." The dead and the desperate "have done things in life that have hurt others." They've "had hurts done to" them. Denton writes, "none of it serves as an excuse." Misogyny rears its ugly head, but there's a rugged kindness too.

Mental healthcare is often out of reach of the dead and the desperate. Denton writes, "In modern America, 20% of mentally ill people do not have access to mental healthcare. It is widely believed that an ineffective mental health network in America is a heavy influence on drug abuse, homelessness, gun violence, domestic violence, prison populations, suicide rates, rates of child abuse, and the exponential growth of the popularity of reality tv. From the beginning of time, until today, the prevailing method mankind has used to deal with mental health is to ignore it, and hope it goes away." Denton goes micro to macro: "You can't walk down no sidewalk in America with only one shoe on and not have the cops show up." A little later on Denton writes, "When you're crazy, you can't be trusted with access to your own thoughts, or genitals." Medications are prescribed and the dead and the desperate must acclimate. The "Prozac hid all the ghosts that danced in my midnights, sure. But it also smothered all the sunshine that sometimes could leak into my rusting heart." The dead and the desperate buckling under the weight of mental illness and destitution turn to whatever substances they can get. It was often a slippery slope down to the bottom; "if you chased the pills long enough, you found the junk. Once you found the junk, you were on a one-way highway to no fucksville, and once you got there, it was next to impossible to go anywhere else. You stayed there until the junk was done with you."

Denton relates the harsh realities of "factory math," where the sum total wipes blood from its fangs, where each worker is just another number smashed into the next until they're reduced to near zero and replaced with a fresh set of digits. Denton writes, "The factory is a marathon of living the same day, the same way every year, until you're too old to stand for 12 hours." Factory math: a Chinese finger trap of unconquerable/incomprehensible situations with imaginary numbers and operations always unbalanced and deep in the red. The dead and the desperate are left out in the cold of the American night trying to fathom the logic of this factory math, a system of control no blue-collar student can ever fully grasp and there are no honest tutors. Yet Denton sings. It might not be a song most find hopeful, Lord knows there's no cheer, but people have been singing the "paycheck to paycheck blues" for as long as this crooked system has been in place. And the blues, despite the ugly, despite the hopelessness, despite the Big Bad Nothing trying to drown out everything with its impending, unending silence, have always been a comfort. The blues have always cajoled a few more heaving pumps from exhausted, dying hearts. Turn the page and listen to the music.

for John Zidarin
who helped me learn
that I am more than
my addictions. RIP John

Sometimes I don't know where
This dirty road is taking me
Sometimes I can't even see the reason why
I guess I keep a-gamblin'
Lots of booze and lots of ramblin'
It's easier than just waitin' around to die

—Townes Van Zandt

1.

I never intended to live in Ohio again in the first place. After my first divorce, and all the ensuing debacles; a rehab here, probation there, a dab or two of homelessness, or years of barely clinging to a roof over my head, and I found myself drunk and alone a lot, watching the free PBS channel in a shitty apartment, in a shitty southern town that had grown just as tired of me as I was of it. I'd been banned from three of the five dive bars that lived in my desperate subdivision of rotting trailer park, slum lord haven, and the other two bars weren't making me feel like I belonged anymore. Sometimes when the moon is full, or when Mercury is in retrograde or some shit, just sometimes I can be hard to get along with I guess. I always seem to get tired of somewhere just as they're getting tired of me, and I was feeling the urge to move again. Seven states in seven years. Might as well find another one.

I was staying home. Drinking alone. So I got the internet in my shitty apartment. I came up with enough scratch to get my phone line turned on, and downloaded one of those 100 hours free CDs.

I was supposed to be a writer someday, and I'd just gotten through 21 of 30 days in another rehab before I had to split. I was working and staying away from the hard shit, and laying low and drinking at home.

I was supposed to be a writer someday, so I'd called this guy some other guy told me about, and that guy came over, and for $20 and an old printer I had, that guy fixed my computer tower up, and debugged it, and got it limping back along again.

I could never afford to keep buying the ink cartridges for the printer, and I hadn't written shit in a long goddamn time, so there wasn't shit ever to print.

I planned to write, and save it on these hard plastic disks, and if I wrote anything worth much, I planned to take the hard disk over to the town library, and use their computer, and print it for a quarter a page.

I don't know what I was going to do with it then, and it didn't matter much. I had the internet in my rat trap apartment, and I was working and keeping my head down. Plenty of money for 12 packs and half decent whiskey once in a while. Plenty of evening time to listen to music on the radio, and write a little, except I never did write much.

The internet then wasn't the internet now. It ran through the phone line, and was slow. There were a lot of naked pictures on the internet, but never any videos. Porn then wasn't like porn now. But there were naked pictures and there were chat rooms. I never wrote much, I just listened to music every night, and looked at naked pictures, and jacked off, and talked dirty in chat rooms, or argued with people in chat rooms, or tried to get women to email me naked pictures if they had a digital camera.

I remember once in high school, this girl I knew sent me a Polaroid picture of her titties in a card once. I had that picture for a long time. But I had the internet in my kitchen-sink-has-been-dripping-since-Reagan was president apartment, and girls could send me naked photos in a matter of minutes to my email, if I could get them to, and sometimes I could.

But jacking off to an unlimited library of nude photos is not the same as fucking, and I could only ever lay low and drink at home for so long before I got bored, and started running around town looking for a good time in all the bad places. I was getting stir crazy.

One weekend I was drunk and bored, and I stayed up all night talking to this chick in a Midwest singles chat room I'd found, and we'd exchanged some emails, and I didn't have a digital camera, but I could type 50 words per minute and I'd spent a lifetime reading books, and you'd be surprised about how far a Neruda stanza can take you in a chat room. Already into the 21st century and most everyone I knew had never heard about ole Pablo Neruda. Quoting poets no one ever heard of makes you seem learned in a 2am internet chat room, and wait til they have a rough day, and you drop some Bukowski on them.

One thing leads to another and I'd just gotten a cell phone for the first time, because I had some money in my pocket and everyone was getting cell phones. Cell phones then were not cell phones now, and mine was about the size of half a brick and didn't send text messages or have a high def screen. It just made phone calls, and those phone calls were free after 7pm and on weekends, so me and this late night chat room girl started calling each other and talking every night, sometimes for hours.

She'd had a few long-term relationships, but nothing had ever come of them, and she'd been single for a while. She was back in college and living at home, and she was fierce and independent, but she was lonely, too, and she didn't really know how to meet people. She was mid 20s and older than most of the college kids in her classes, and her job as an activities coordinator at a local nursing home offered nary a bed warmer, either.

She'd had a few Friday night one-night stands, from going to one of the half-assed dance clubs cities in the Midwest they're always trying to keep open, but that wasn't enough.

She liked to fuck she said, and I told her I did, too.

Next thing you know she's driving down south, and I'm taking a four-day weekend. We drove around to different places to eat every evening, but mostly we drank and we fucked. We fucked and fucked all weekend, like you do when you just meet somebody that likes to fuck in all the same ways you like to fuck, and neither of you have fucked much lately. If you don't understand that last sentence, I hope you figure it out before you die. It is one of the most magical things I have experienced in my sad ass life, and chasing those weekends has nearly ruined me, and killed me a dozen times over.

Lover girl goes home, and we keep talking late at night, me half drunk all the time, and her just lonely. She drinks, but she doesn't understand why I need to drink every day, and all the time, but I work hard, and "I miss you" and "I miss you, too" and the fucking, that was some of the best fucking ever, and maybe I'll just drive up to Ohio one weekend and we can fuck six times a day again for four days. See how quick I forgot about hating Ohio? That's how women have always worked for me.

I can't fully explain it, except for the obvious, being a fucked up dude trying to survive a fucked up life. It's what we do. We drink and fuck and fight. You see us on Cops and Jerry Springer every day.

Before I could get back up there to do all that fucking again, lover girl calls me and says she's pregnant.

2.

In all my years of chaos, I had never given much thought about ever being a Dad. Sure, there'd been some close calls, and two abortions, but I'd never considered what I would do if I became a Dad. I was too busy all the time chasing women, and when I got one, they didn't stay around long. Parts of me hoped I would find someone that would stick around, but other parts of me didn't care so much, as long as there wasn't too much of a gap between girls.

I knew it wasn't normal probably to be that way. That's another thing about being fucked up, most of us know we're fucked up, but sometimes it works and sometimes it doesn't, whether you're fucked up or not.

Whether it was normal, or not, to be the way I was then, it's how I was. Right, wrong, good and bad, don't ever change the truth about things no matter what the news channels and politicians try to feed us.

When the chat room girl had come down to visit, and when we'd done all that fucking, we'd started out using condoms the first few times, but we were out pacing what was left in the box on my night stand. I tried to be good about using condoms and being careful, but after the 5th or 6th time we fucked she said she didn't care. That was all the green light I needed.

Once you fuck a girl without a condom, you're never going to want to wear another one with her again. If you don't understand that, I hope you figure it out before you die. But after that, neither of us ever mentioned condoms again that weekend, and I'm sure I was pulling out and shit, but one thing you can take to the bank, the most devastating bad decisions I ever made in life involved fucking and women, and I'd made a lot of bad fucking decisions by the time I'd met the chat room girl.

Now, five weeks after all that, and she called and said she was pregnant.

"You sure," I said. I'd gotten this phone call a few times before, and half the time they weren't pregnant. I was already crossing my fingers.

"I was late, so I went and bought two tests this morning. They're both positive" she said, and in that moment there was a lot of unspoken things going on between interstate cell phone towers that I maybe still don't understand, even today. But when you have one of them phone calls, you can sure as shit trust that it's a different outlook on both sides of the telephone.

Lucky I'd been through this situation before, and even being a stubborn slow learner, I'd learned what not to do in moments like this. I knew this chat room girl didn't see a positive test from my viewpoint. I hope you've never had to consider fatherhood from that viewpoint. It wasn't pleasant considerations.

So I waited til all the scared parts of me settled and what I said was, "Alright. I guess I need to come soon so we can figure out what to do."

What she said next is one of the bigger reasons why you should probably talk this over before you knock someone up, but it was done and here we were.

"What do you mean what to do? If I'm pregnant, I'm pregnant. I don't believe in abortion," she said, and all the scared parts of me churned up so hard again that my heart almost stopped a minute. But I kept it together, and never let on about the cyclone raging in my heart, but that phone call didn't have any elements of fucking in it.

Not the kind of fucking I was forever chasing, but maybe some of the fucking I was always trying to avoid in life. Either way, I packed up some clothes in a bag, grabbed a couple of books, and headed back north to visit Ohio, a place that I had lied to myself about never going back to, and when I got back to Ohio, I never left again, and I'm still here even though I never intended to be.

3.

When I finally drove back up north to Ohio to see about what to do,
I had a whole lot of road trip hours to think about all of it. It didn't
help. Sometimes thinking is good, and sometimes you just gotta show
up to see how it goes. And it went. I intended to hang out and see
what we were going to do, and I never went back south to get the rest
of my stuff. I got a factory job that first week. It paid $15 an hour
which is better than what the factories were paying in the south, but
the factory had rotating 12-hour shifts, which also meant a lot of
overtime.

We got a little one-bedroom apartment, and we moved in together
on the 8th day we'd spent together in person. Sure, we'd talked on
the phone for two months, and there was a part of me that knew that
this was a pretty wild situation, but I couldn't figure anything else
out to do about it, so I bought a 12 pack every day and drank it in
a tiny living room in a lazy boy recliner as old as I was and passed
down from her grandmother's basement. My new girlfriend who was
pregnant sat on an ugly, but cozy loveseat we'd got at the Goodwill
for $20. We'd talk. Watch cable TV. We had to have cable TV so she
could watch her programs, and she liked to watch a lot of programs.
Some of them were ok, but most I didn't care too much about because
I had ever only had cable TV when I lived in cheap $100-A-Week
Motels, so I barely ever watched TV unless football was on, or
PBS had a good Austin City Limits guest on, or if PBS had a good
documentary sometimes, too. She didn't care if I read a book while
she watched her programs, so mostly I did, and I drank a 12 pack, and
we'd go to bed at the same time, and we fucked every night, and the
fucking was good. And I'd pass out a little drunk and a lot tired from

12 factory hours which are 1.5 times heavier than ordinary hours everywhere else, so carrying them makes you 1.5 times more tired every night, even though you sleep 1.5 times less because your body is not made to work a factory shift. It's factory math. I've been figuring on it and at it, for a lot of years, and it's close enough to true that you'll have a hard time finding a factory worker that disagrees.

My second week in the factory was my first on the 12-hour night shift, and despite all of my 50+ jobs in life, I have never successfully worked a night shift. But I stayed up after work one morning, and me and my new girlfriend that was pregnant went to see the doctor together.

She was sure as shit pregnant. About seven weeks, and the doctor and the nurse did some math that isn't factory math, and we were gonna be parents in about seven and a half months was their best guess.

The girlfriend was pretty happy about all this it seemed, and I was trying to figure out what to do. We went and got some lunch at a Big Boy diner after and she asked not to sit in the smoking section. I understood that, so we didn't, but I hadn't been to bed yet. When you're tired, a cup of coffee without a cigarette is just a cup of coffee, and I was kind of pissed about it. She could tell, even though I didn't say anything, in that way you can always feel when someone is irritated.

"We can go sit over there," she said, reaching across the table to grab both of my hands in hers.

"No." I said. "It's alright. I gotta get used to it." That made her smile, and that was ok I guess. When we got home, I drank a big glass of crown royal and Pepsi, and my new girlfriend that was sure as shit pregnant and happy about it rewarded me for staying up all day with a pretty good blow job.

Then I passed out for three hours before work.

When I got up, I was running late, so I stopped at the corner gas station for 2 cheeseburgers for $3 from the hot rack, 2 packs of smokes, and 2 tall boys of Natty Light. I made it to the factory on time with both beers gone, and the cheeseburgers ready to eat on the fly. Somehow, that was enough to get me through another deadman's graveyard shift.

4.

I found this dive bar halfway between the factory and my tiny-could-use a doormat as-a-throw-rug apartment that was growing smaller by the week. The bar was called the Bucket in those days. It's closed now. Bulldozed down to build a parking lot for a giant new super Wal-Mart that has its own zip code. There's no tombstone. The Bucket's just another ghost bulldozed by capitalism; another landmark erased by the machine.

It wasn't much of a bar anyway. A small block building painted black, that changed its t-shirt every week, thanks to local graffiti artists with pockets full of spray paint cans and heads full of pop-hip-hop.

The Bucket had a bar with about a dozen stools and a couple of hand me down tables with adopted chairs rescued from yard sales. In the back, there was a scruffy pool table that hadn't washed his face in three years and a beat to hell jukebox that always seemed like it could use a nap.

The best thing about the Bucket was they were grandfathered in with a liquor license that allowed them to open at 5am, two hours before most other bars. You could get a mason jar draft beer for a buck til noon, seven days a week, and for a buck and half after that til 2:30am. Then they closed the doors so they could mop the floors before opening back up to serve breakfast to those that preferred to drink it.

I started stopping at the Bucket after work some days. Especially when I was on the night shift. The pregnant girlfriend liked to sleep til about 9 or 9:30, and night shift got out at 6am, so I'd stop and spend $20 to get beer drunk and listen to tired songs from a jukebox that yawned between sets.

12

5.

Me and my pregnant girlfriend went to the doctor again. Congrats. It's a girl. The girlfriend reacted like she'd won a *Price is Right* showcase, except she didn't jump up and down. She covered her face, cried and laughed at the same time, and said "I've always wanted a little girl." That's another thing you should maybe talk about prior to starting a family. Do both parties want to start a family? That's an important topic. Too late for it now.

During her fifth month pregnant, we screamed at each other for five hours one night because she wanted me to quit smoking in the apartment. I told her she was welcome to go outside when I smoked if she didn't like it. I didn't mean it, but it didn't matter, because we were on edge all the time. We were planning a family, shopping for little girl clothes, little white Nike shoes with a pink swoosh. Putting together a baby shower wish list, and ooh, that's a nice crib, and we're gonna have to get a 2-bedroom apartment eventually. It's only an extra $250 a month. How about these invitations, and we gotta get her dedicated at church. Dedicated!?! Church? You believe in God? You don't? Oh, shit, we were doing this and we didn't even fucking know each other.

We screamed at each other for five hours until the cops came and knocked on the apartment door like cops always knock. The pregnant girlfriend looked a mess. She'd been crying for five hours and screaming. She was hoarse and exhausted, and I had not shed a single tear. I wasn't hoarse at all, even though I had sure as shit yelled for five motherfucking hours, too. The one that yells the loudest and the longest wins the argument. That's what my parents taught me.

There were two cops. Then four cops. Then four fucking cop cars with cop lights, calling all the Jell-O-brained neighbors to peek out their windows. I was led out to sit handcuffed on the curb while they consoled my emotionally exhausted girlfriend who couldn't stop crying long enough to tell these combat boot wearing cops what the fuck was going on.

All we did was yell at each other and say mean things. What crime is that?

Turns out isn't a crime to yell and say mean things. Cops are still cops. An older fat cop, with a doughnut belly so big that you couldn't even see his gun-belt, gave me a little lecture on not drinking so much. Said maybe I should learn to not be a piece of shit that yells and says mean things to pregnant girlfriends.

I said, "Sure thing captain," or some shit.

They asked if I had somewhere I could go for the night. I resisted any talk of his mother's house.

I've had a long and adventurous history with authority. I've gotten better at keeping my mouth shut over the years. Talking shit is second only to chasing pussy on the list of ways I've found to fuck up my own life.

I didn't say shit to the fat doughnut belly cop. I just told him no.

How could I have somewhere to go? I'd lied to myself and wound up back in Ohio. Back to factory rust and dive bar lust.

The cops took me to a downtown shelter and told me not to go back home til morning, or else they'd take me to jail. Or some shit. My head hurt, and now I was pissed.

All this, over a motherfucking cigarette.

6.

I was pissed at the pregnant girlfriend, even though she hadn't been the one that called the cops. It didn't matter. I was fucking pissed.

I waited til the cops drove away, and I walked to the edge of downtown where there was a $29-a-night, lowlife motel. It was for lowlifes, like me, because I was certain that no good decisions had been made in this motel, no matter how many Bibles the Gideons crammed down our throats.

The night clerk was a Middle Eastern man who didn't believe in deodorant, and the entire lobby smelled like cooked, foreign foods. There was a large poster behind the desk. It had a big American flag and a Christian cross. It said "Proud to be American. God Bless the U.S.A." Some words say more than they think they do.

I stayed at the motel for four days, because I was fucking pissed. I didn't call the pregnant girlfriend. I didn't go to work. I went to the liquor store, and I locked myself in my room, and I got fucked up. I watched stupid daytime TV, and plastic hit-sitcom-laugh tracks in the evening.

I went for a walk. There was a woman in short shorts and a tube top at the corner by the 24- hour Big Boy Diner. She was probably 35, but her odometer wasn't highway miles. They were backseat, crack pipe miles. She looked 50.

"You know where we can get some rock?" I asked her, and she did. We walked to this house a few blocks into a neighborhood that didn't believe in streetlights. She went in while I stood on the sidewalk debating whether I was afraid of the dark.

She got two dimes for $30, because she owed him from being short last time. Simple street economics.

The woman stayed in the lowlife motel with me and we did not make any good decisions that night. She left in the morning, and it was just me, two bottles of $6 whiskey, cable TV, and the Gideon Bible. Impossible to make good decisions under this kind of duress.

I stayed for four days, because my money ran out on the fifth morning.

I walked back home to the tiny apartment because I didn't have any money for a cab, and I was too proud, and too stupid to call anyone and ask for a ride. I was wearing the same clothes I was wearing since I left five nights ago, and I hadn't showered.

The pregnant girlfriend was relieved to see me, but I felt like hell. The way hell is going to feel for Republican governors someday. That level of hell. I took four aspirin with jack straight out of a half bottle I'd left on top of the fridge a week ago. I drank some jack in the shower. Straight. This wasn't for pleasure. The hot water almost felt human.

I told the pregnant girlfriend she had to get the doctor to sign a paper saying I was taking care of her so I wouldn't get in trouble for missing five days of work.

She didn't want to lie to her doctor. She didn't like to lie. It had to be done, and she did it, and I ain't happy or proud of it.

I had a new boss at the factory. He was Mormon, and big on family. I gave him the doctor note, and he took care of my attendance, and I was back singing the paycheck-to-paycheck blues.

I only smoked in the apartment when she wasn't around. She still bitched, but what're you gonna do? The cops can only hassle a man for smoking in his own apartment so many times, before they get bored and move on to real crime, like shaking down weed smokers, and hassling panhandlers.

About 2 weeks after the big argument, I got a call from the front office at the factory while I was out on the factory floor sweating and grinding. They said someone from the hospital called. My girlfriend was there.

I left the factory and drove over to the hospital with a storm front of emotions raining all over me.

She'd had some contractions or something, and the baby's heart rate was either too fast, or too slow. They sent the girlfriend home ordered to bed rest.

She blamed it on me, and karma for making her lie to the doctor, and didn't talk to me for three days. It goes like that sometimes with women. You get blamed for shit that don't make sense to you much, then you can't ask questions about it. You're just supposed to know. I have rarely known, but mostly accepted that I fucked around, and fucked up so much shit all the time that I might as well accept the blame and keep it moving.

The girlfriend couldn't work, and she wasn't making much planning activities for the residents at the old folk's home, but that meant that my factory hours were the only thing keeping the apartment roof over our heads.

The pregnant girlfriend couldn't work, and she didn't have health insurance since planning old folk's activities only required part time work. One day, while I was boots on the concrete, in factory purgatory, the girlfriend's mom took the girlfriend to the welfare office. She signed up for Medicaid for her, and the baby, and for the WIC program for milk, cheese, and juice, and a food stamp card.

"Food stamps come on a bank card?" I asked the pregnant girlfriend.

She looked at me strange.

"They used to come in a booklet and looked like Monopoly money," I told her.

"Oh," she said.

Sometimes I forget that not everyone grows up in the projects.

I started picking up extra shifts at the factory after the girlfriend couldn't work. I was working 6-12 hour shifts a week, and stopping at the Bucket, or going home to watch tv and drink beer, and sleep, and get head once in a while, since we'd been told we should maybe hold back on the fucking for a bit.

Work was work, and the days kept sliding away into the night, and the weeks strung together. I was falling behind on the books that I wanted to read, and I still didn't write shit. Except in one notebook, six pages of scribble, and one half decent, half poem. I only took one day off every two weeks. The one day before the shifts swung the other direction.

One night, after another kick-in-the-dick, 12-hour night shift, a couple of the guys from work went to the Bucket with me, and we drank beers, traded rounds of shots, and told stories til noon.

I'd left my cell phone in the car, and when I got in the car, I saw I'd missed about 15 phone calls.

Shit.

When I got home the pregnant girlfriend was sitting in our tiny living room with her mom. Her mom worked as a cashier at a flower shop. She'd worked there for years.

"Where the hell have you been?" the pregnant girlfriend yelled.

"At the bar" I said, and I walked past them into our bedroom and started taking my clothes off to shower.

"You couldn't call!?!" I heard her yell at my back.

I was down to my boxers when I saw the pregnant girlfriend standing in the doorway of the bedroom. Her mom was standing behind her with her eyes real big, and angry looking. I took my boxers off and walked naked to the bathroom off the bedroom and shut the door.

I got the shower going, and the pregnant girlfriend came in and sat on the toilet. She was half yelling about shit, so I yanked the shower curtain open to invite her in. Figured she could wash my back, while she bitched.

The pregnant girlfriend's mom was standing in the doorway with her arms crossed. If looks could kill I'd never have another hard on, but I did. And I was drunk and water was spraying everywhere, so I did the only thing I could think to do; I helicoptered my hard on.

The pregnant girlfriend's mom gasped, and stomped off, but the pregnant girlfriend tried to cover a laugh. We heard the tiny apartment's front door slam, and me and the pregnant girlfriend both laughed for two minutes. When we were done laughing I helicoptered again a little, and the pregnant girlfriend laughed for a second. Then she leaned forward, and took me in her mouth, and neither of us much cared that the shower was still spraying all over. I was drunk, and for eight minutes I didn't care about anything.

7.

The pregnant girlfriend was still pregnant, and still my girlfriend. We had a little pile of the stuff you collect before babies are born, piled up in one corner of our one bedroom. I was working, sleeping, eating, getting drunk before, and after work, going to the bar sometimes, and sometimes getting head when I got home.

That was the pregnant girlfriend's go to move. I'd be drunk, and half dead from working twice as many hours than I slept every week, and she'd be doing stuff that got on my nerves. She'd stop what she was doing and suck my dick. Worked every time. It's hard to find a lot to bitch about after all your dreams have just been sucked out of you. The pregnant girlfriend would get up and get us both a Kleenex. Then she'd go back to doing whatever it was she was doing that annoyed me before. Except I didn't care anymore. I didn't think that this was love, but after one of those really great head sessions after a long night shift, I remember drifting off to sleep thinking this wasn't so bad really.

The pregnant girlfriend and her mother had resumed meeting around our dining room table. We had gotten the table and four chairs for $75 from the classifieds in the newspaper.

They were meeting around the table a lot, and writing things in notebooks, and talking about a baby shower. I was on the two week-dayshift swing of our swinging shifts. They'd both be there after I stopped at the bar for a few medicinal rounds, to keep me numb enough, to keep me from quitting this life. The pregnant girlfriend's mother never said a word to me. That said enough.

One night I came home about 2 hours after work, and I was hungry. I asked what we were doing for dinner. That's all I asked, and her mom huffed, but the pregnant girlfriend didn't say anything. So I said OK, guess I'll go get something to eat then, or something. Her Mom said something about me always drinking my dinner, and I said who gives a fuck and the girlfriend was crying. The mom sat there red faced and mad, then huffed again, and got up and kissed her daughter. She told her to call her later and she gave me looks she wished were killing looks, all the way to the apartment door.

The pregnant girlfriend was still crying, and I wished she would stop. I was tired as fuck, and only a little drunk. I was hungry, and I wanted to shower, and eat, and get more drunk. If that went ok, maybe get a little head, before falling asleep for 5 fucking hours, and doing it all over again. Was that too much to ask?

Turns out it was.

"You don't ever want to come home and spend time with me," she said.

I said some things about winding down from factory life. She said I could come home and tell her and drink at home with her. I said some things about not wanting to hang out with her mom all the time and that set her off. I said some mean things and she said some mean things. That wasn't a fair fight because I didn't much care about having mean things said to me. There wasn't a lot to say that hurt my feelings. I'd known I was fucked up for a long time by the time she got around to telling me. Plus, she wasn't telling me anything I hadn't heard, from other women, in other living rooms, much like this one.

We yelled for a while, and she cried some more. Then we were done, and I was too sober. We ordered a pizza, and some breadsticks, and I cracked a beer. We sat on the loveseat together, and we turned the tv on just like everyone else in America. I drank some beers, and we ate pizza, and went to bed.

The pregnant girlfriend had one brother, and he lived in Dayton. He worked drawing blueprints for some engineering company. He was older than the pregnant girlfriend, and he was married with one kid.

Him and his wife drove up one Saturday, and I took the day off. We were all at the pregnant girlfriend's parents' house.

The pregnant girlfriend's brother was trading stock tips with the pregnant girlfriend's dad. The three of us were standing in the back yard holding beers and watching meat sizzle on a grill.

The pregnant girlfriend, and her mom, and her sister-in-law were sitting at a patio table. The mom had a notebook out, and they were talking about babies, and baby showers.

The pregnant girlfriend's nephew was about five years old, and he was running around the backyard looking for bugs to stomp, and ant hills to kick over. He screamed a lot while he ran around, and nobody else seemed to care that he was running around screaming, and stomping on bugs, but I was starting to care. My beer was empty, and I got another one. The pregnant girlfriend's brother was talking about golf putters. The meat was still sizzling. Kid still screaming.

"What do you do?" the brother asked me when the father started flipping the meat over with a four-foot spatula that bore the emblem of a college university.

"I work at the factory," I said.

"What do you do there?" he asked.

"Run the machine." I said.

"Oh. I thought maybe you were in management. My sister said you were smart."

That hung in the air for a half a beer.

Then he asked what I was into, and that caught me off-guard. I hadn't expected an interview.

"I like books," I shrugged.

"Oh. What kind of books?"

"Poetry. Some novels. I read that new John Grisham book. Your sister got it for me at the grocery store. It was alright."

"Oh. You ever read the Christian rapture series? My smoking hot wife loves those. I don't read too much. Just golf digest, and a "I Wish I was Rich Monthly Magazine.""

"They got any poems in the golf digest?" I asked him.

He shook his head.

"Golf is its own poetry," he said, and swung his one arm in a half golf swing. We both turned to watch the imaginary half golf ball crash through a neighbor's window.

The father was done flipping meat on the grill, and that saved me. The brother started talking about the economy, and my beer was empty again. I went and got another one from the fridge in the garage. I could feel the drops of sweat on my forehead scribbling messages in a bottle. Help. Who are these people?

It got worse after we ate the overcooked meat that had sizzled for too long. The pregnant girlfriend was in the living room laying on the couch, and I was stuck outside with everyone else. The Dad and the brother decided to play baseball with the terrorist five-year-old, and they had a big red plastic bat and a plastic ball. They were out in the yard trying to teach the little fucker how to hold a bat if you hit right-handed, but the dad and the brother couldn't agree on where you put your hands on the bat to hit right-handed.

The sister-in-law said to me, "You guys think of any names?" And that was a stupid thing to say. We'd spent half of dinner talking about baby names.

The sister-in-law was 30 and working hard to stay in her 20s and she was doing pretty good at it.

"I voted for Mary, after Jesus' Mom," I shrugged.

The pregnant girlfriend's mom hmphed.

"She gonna have your last name?" the sister-in-law said.

"Yes," I said. And the pregnant girlfriend's mom hmphed again.

The five-year-old yanked the big red bat away, and it hit his dad in the nuts pretty good. The Dad crab walked around, hunched over, and trying to breathe the way you do when you get cracked in the sack, and I spit beer laughing about it. His hot wife hid a smile, too. The dude's mom went out and made sure her son was ok.

The pregnant girlfriend's mother made homemade ice cream for dessert in some mop bucket looking machine. Everyone sat around the back patio saying how much they loved homemade ice cream. They all had seconds. I didn't have any ice cream; I just got another beer.

When me and the pregnant girlfriend were driving back to our human storage unit apartment, she said that I'd done well, and her brother said I was quiet, but seemed ok.

"That's a good thing. You're gonna want him on your side." She'd said.

Yay, team I thought.

8.

They sometimes call the factory "the plant."

It's because they plant work boots on concrete.

They plant empty dreams in human hearts.

They plant blood and sweat and arthritis

They plant broken homes in local communities
and hang climate change in all our broken windows

They plant addiction, anxiety and stress
and dance marionette cruise ship faux-cations in front of our dimming
eyes.

They plant bankruptcies and reverse mortgages
and they plant cancer
in every organ
in every cell
in the air
and the water
and in the earth.

They call the factory a motherfucking plant because they sure as shit
plant cancer
and they plant it
and plant it
and plant it

and it eats at us

it eats at our city budgets
it eats our schools
and our children
and our futures

and when all the cancer that they've planted has eaten all of the laughter of our children's children, the factory will turn its back and leave to plant cancer in China, and Mexico, and Vietnam, and Taiwan and India.

They call the factory the plant because it's where they plant the American Dream, and they fertilize the American Dream with American Workers that give half their lives to grow money for Wall Street Farmers, and that money is funneled to 10 Billionaires that own all the land the factory plants and factory workers live and die on.

9.

Me and the pregnant girlfriend got in a big fight. It all stemmed from a misunderstanding. She thought I was the kind of guy that would go to a baby shower, and she was wrong. That argument lasted for six days, and five nights. We took breaks for me to check in at the factory, then resumed as soon as I got home from the Bucket. When the dust settled on our little 10-year war, we stood at an impasse. She carried a banner that said I'd go to my daughter's baby shower, and I wore a T shirt that said she had me fucked up.

"You obviously aren't ready to be an adult," she said.

And I replied, "Bitch, I don't even know your middle name."

Turns out it was Rose.

The fight lasted six days and five nights because I went to work on the sixth night. At some point during that 12-hour factory shift, and sometime during the four hours after, when I sat on a barstool looking for answers in the bucket, the pregnant girlfriend called a truce during those 16 hours, and I came home to an empty tiny apartment. Most of the furniture was still there, but all of the pregnant girlfriend's clothes were gone. The pile of stuff you collect before babies show up was gone. Her shampoo and conditioner and 11 bottles of soaps were gone from the shower shelf. Her toothbrush was gone from the plastic toothbrush cup holder that sat on the bathroom sink.

She'd left the liquor on top of the fridge, and I was glad for that. I opened a half bottle of Jameson's that I'd splurged and bought two weeks ago when I got my first 45 cent raise in the factory. I'd drank half the bottle that night because Jameson's is easy to drink, then decided to save the rest for another time to celebrate.

This didn't feel like a time of celebration, but it also wasn't a time of death. It was purgatory, and nobody much can endure the weight of waiting.

The only radio I could find in this supposed home of mine was a $10, Dollar Store clock radio, and that made me blue, so I drank some Jameson's. I brought the clock radio, that was hardly a radio at all, into the living room, that was hardly a living room. I found a local rock channel with minimal static, and too many commercials, and I drank some more Jameson's.

10.

The American factory didn't always just grow money for Wall Street farmers.

Once upon a time, a few cancer sowing, cancer growing rich white guys, built great sprawling factories. Those rich white guys were so riddled with the cancer of greed that they kidnapped village children and made them work 16-hour shifts for their dinner.

Those rich white guys that built the sprawling American factories, hired private armies to protect those factories. Many American workers were murdered to insure compliance.

Then some liberal folks that are often referred to as socialists, harnessed the growing desperation of American workers, who were working for only half a dinner at this point, and that's if they could beg and scratch enough to find work, and those socialists rode that solidarity of desperation to a working, thriving middle class.

Once upon a time a company CEO only made 20 times as much as the man running his machines. And the American Dream was planted and it grew. The American Dream grew, but it still had cancers, and warts, and 13 other diseases you can find in the dictionary but are hard to pronounce. The American Dream was born with cancer because it grew from constitutional promises born of lies, and it grew from two of the biggest cancers of them all: religion and racism.

The American Dream grew because these socialist unions marched, and marched, and they shouted clever slogans. They worked to keep the American factory in the business of growing the American Dream, and not just money for Wall Street farmers.

Once upon a time the American Dream grew in plants called factories, the American Dream bore fruit, and the American worker ate well, and subdivisions were born around working cities.

The American Dream grew sprouts of a future for the children of the American worker, and colleges sprouted revolutions that grew change, until the Vietnam War sucked up all the change in agent orange clouds that stole whole generations of youth and futures from American Workers. The American Dream grew until the Vietnam War ground the Dream to a stump, chipping away at the Dream by selecting random teenaged boys from every town in America, then feeding those teenaged boys to a war machine that spit out their names. You can find those names engraved on black granite plaques in small towns scattered all across Woody Guthrie's America.

A war machine named Vietnam ate up all the dreams and futures of small-town America. A different war machine named fascism smashed dreams of revolution in Chicago 1968.

In Chicago 1968, the revolution that was planted at Colleges and Universities had grown just as the American Dream had grown. The revolution held a prayer circle in Chicago 1968, but an army of cops and National Guardsmen, all of whom were our next-door neighbors who only played warrior on the weekends. An army of our very next-door neighbors, who enjoyed the same fruit from the same American Dream, those fuckers drowned the American Dream in an ocean of an agent orange called tear gas.

Then a man with no moral compass was born, and he became president. His name was Richard Nixon, and he lied to everyone and said he was not a crook. That motherfucker was indeed a crook, and he tried to strangle the American Dream all by himself.

Then an actor that snitched to Congress about other actors got to be president. His name was Ronald Reagan, and he broke the legs of the socialist unions, and he started auctioning off American factories to the lowest bidders across the world, to places where dreams don't grow.

A no-good man named Ronald Reagan, destroyed the roots of the American Dream that used to grow in American factories, and lobbyists bought the politicians, and with no roots down, the American Dream didn't stand a chance. It blew away in great Grapes of Wrath dust bowls called Savings and Loan, George W. Bush and stolen elections, 20-year wars on manufactured terrorism, recessions, and reality TV.

In a barren wasteland, post Ronald Reagan America, the CEO makes 300 times more than the worker on the machine, and the three wealthiest men in America own half the country.

In a barren wasteland, post Ronald Reagan America, American factories are called plants because they grow money for Wall Street farmers who don't even bother to leave black granite plaques with the names of those it's eaten alive.

11.

When I came home to the tiny empty apartment, I drank the Jameson's, and I listened to rock music. When the Jameson's was gone I started in on a two-thirds bottle of Jack, and I fiddled with the Dollar Store clock radio that barely passed as a radio, and I found a classic rock channel.

They played "The Ballad of Curtis Loew," by Lynyrd Skynyrd at about 1 in the morning. My heart might have smiled if it wasn't stuck in purgatory, and looking for answers in an empty bottle of Jack.

When the sun came up, I'd been up for 36 hours or some shit, and I opened a bottle of $6 vodka I'd bought once to make martinis, but I'd never found a reason to make martinis in the tiny apartment. I have never cared for martinis, but I'd worked as a side hustle bartender before, and knowing the best routes to get to fuckedupsville is something I'd developed a knack for, and just in case someone visited the tiny apartment and had a thirst for a martini, then I was fucking prepared, man.

Never had a reason to make martinis, but I had the vodka, so I poured some in a glass and drank it straight and room temperature. It tasted like paint thinner, so I drank it a little quicker so I wouldn't have to taste it as much. I fingered the Dollar Store clock radio some more and wondered how they expected the thing to play music when it didn't have any heart. They stopped manufacturing appliances with hearts because making things with heart cost too much, and poor factory workers in tiny apartments didn't have any money to spend on unnecessary heart. They've always had to find their own.

The local public radio channel was playing classical music, and it didn't have any commercials, so I left it there to trickle out of the back of the clock radio, and I looked out the window of my apartment until I didn't know what I was looking at and finally, I fell asleep on the living room floor. It was dark when I woke up, and my face hurt like carpet burn.

After drinking for two days straight, I felt like I had cottonmouth of the brain and my mouth was so dry that my teeth all had migraines.

All I could find to treat the dried up, crusty sponge of a heart that I had left, was two bottles of Red Stripe beer in the back of an empty fridge that had depression issues. The Red Stripes had sat orphaned for so long they'd started turning bitter from their rejection.

I couldn't find any toothpaste because the pregnant girlfriend had claimed custody of the only toothpaste tube in the tiny apartment. I poured Red Stripe over my toothbrush and shined my face up as best I could.

I went outside to go to the liquor store. It was the middle of the day, and the sun screamed white, high-definition-light on all the world's outsides. My eyes were still wearing dark living room cataracts, and the sun hurt my feelings.

I got enough supplies at the liquor dispensary to get me through a few more days, and I bought a three-piece fried chicken dinner from a place owned by a Kentucky military man.

My stomach was hungover from a 72-hour vacation and was not awake enought to enjoy fried chicken. I puked at a stop sign, then got home and drank a little. The stomach came back around with an apology letter. Lucky, that fried chicken and biscuits are good as fuck, even when they're cold.

I was deep in a big bottle of poor man's whiskey, when the pregnant girlfriend let herself in with the key. The $10, dollar store clock radio was dying, and half of the music notes it was supposed to play were coming out as tv static. The pregnant girlfriend switched off the heartless radio, and I let her take my hand and lead me to bed.

She was gentle, and soft, which was too much for the barbed wire that was growing around my chain-link heart, and I was melting in her mouth in ways that felt so good that it might have been love.

But it wasn't. It was just warmth, and softness, and a mouth that could almost make a man believe in Heaven.

I woke up a day later, and the pregnant girlfriend was still laying next to me, naked and big and soft and warm. My hands read Braille lust letters, and the pregnant girlfriend that I didn't know I wanted, used her mouth to tell me that she didn't think this was love either. She used her mouth to tell me that Heaven might be real. And she showed me. And I was willing to agree that 10 minutes of Heaven was better than a lifetime in purgatory.

12.

After another lost week of living with a heart that had lost his roadmap, I went back to the factory. The factory is true north for blue collar hearts.

I went in a little early, and almost sober. I got the Mormon boss off to himself, and I was almost honest about what was going on. I laid it on, about how I was doing my best to figure out how to be a dad, and a family man, after a whole mid-20s life of never having one single decent role model for how you were supposed to be a good dad.

I left out the part about how I was lost about how to do this with a pregnant girlfriend that I barely knew, and was beginning to suspect that I did not enjoy as much as those first four days of our fuck-cation had led me to believe I did.

I left that part out on account of the boss man being a Mormon, and I don't mean to make it appear that I gave a fuck then, or now, about how he celebrates the magic of our world. I didn't then, and I don't now. I've tried my best to be even keeled about how much labels mean when I consider whether I enjoy someone, or not. I have failed at it a lot.

The Mormon boss was one of the kindest humans I've ever met in a factory, and with any amount of thought I'll admit that the Mormons I've known have all been kind to me. I'd prefer they not recruit for their brand of magic worship at my front door, and they do have some wild fucking ideas about the magic. I've read their book. I found it for a quarter at a small-town thrift store, and I threw it away after I'd read it cover to cover, and then picked at it a bit to make sure I had an outline of what it was they were recruiting about. That was many years ago, and I couldn't give you a fair assessment of their idea of the magic, but I'll tell you, their sacred book has some pretty fucking unbelievable science fiction elements in it.

I threw that book away because John Prine taught me one of the wisest lessons a guru has ever taught. It's in the holy catalogue of John Prine scripture, chapter two, where the guru teaches "try and find Jesus on your own." I've tried and failed, and tried and failed, at not telling people where he's not. People do not like hearing you tell them he's not where they have always been told he is, but I knew he wasn't there, so I threw the book away, and started looking somewhere else. I've tried not to care if anyone understood.

The Mormon boss man was too kind and gentle to be a boss man, and we all knew it, but I was a fucked up drunk. No matter how many good intentions I had, I also had a tiny apartment with a too big rent, and utilities that the apartment-land office manager wouldn't let me live without, even though I had often lived without them. Those utilities I had to have, cost more money than I could afford to pay, most of the time.

That's the thing about most factory workers. We can't take a day off work without some planning, and we damn sure can't afford to get fired because we can't go weeks without a paycheck. That's what happens when you get fired in the factory. Getting a job next week, no matter how good, or bad, will minimize those weeks to about three, and falling three weeks behind takes three years to catch up. It's factory math, and I'd already earned my degree in factory math by 25. So, I laid it on thick to the Mormon boss man about how hard it was to try to be a family man in this crazy world.

I got called down to talk to a night shift Human Resources lady, and she was not as nice as the Mormon boss. She told me I'd better get my shit together. She said she was tired of seeing my name in her company emails. She said that one more strike, and I was out, and I'd be fired, and falling farther behind.

13.

Joe ran the machine behind mine at the factory. Me and Joe both fixed up little bootleg break areas behind our machines, because the closest break area was a hundred fucking yards away.

We both used plastic parts totes and made make-shift chairs. I had a little microwave that I'd inherited from another dude that used to run Joe's machine. That dude got shit-canned for missing too much work. He left his microwave, so I took it, and put it on a hydraulic tank behind my machine. The microwave was filthy, and covered with machine dust, and factory cancer, but we kept the inside of it spotless.

With his machine behind mine, our DIY private break areas were next to each other. We sat back there behind our machines, and smoked cigarettes, and talked shit, when it was break time, or when 'forklift Bob' fell asleep on his Hilo fork truck again and was late bringing us fresh parts to feed the hungry machines.

Joe was in his late 20s, short and stocky like me. He was going bald too young, so he wore hats every day. Trucker style ones in the summer, and wool beanie style ones in the winter.

Joe lived 45 minutes away from the factory in bumfucksville, OH. Population 800. He had 4 kids, and a wife at home. They'd had their first kid at 17 and gotten married. Joe loved his wife, and he took damn good care of his kids. Always going to Tee-ball games, and perfect attendance kindergarten graduations and shit.

His wife only worked part-time, collecting rents 20 hours a week at a small, middle of the country trailer park.

Joe and I spent more time together than we did with our families, whether our families wanted us to, or not. 12 hours a day, most every day. We got to be pretty tight after a few months of singing the cancer dust factory blues together.

Joe was a crazy country boy that liked to drink cheap beer out of the can. Even at the Bucket, he didn't drink the dollar drafts.

"It tastes better in a can. It's colder," he said.

"What the fuck ever," I said.

Joe liked to drink just as much as I liked to drink, and he sold drugs. He'd learned it from his dad, who'd learned it from his dad, who learned it by moonshining in eastern Kentucky.

"You learn to get by," Joe said.

Me and Joe were drinking up at the Bucket that morning after the bitchy HR lady bitched me out.

"Dude. You got 9 lives." Joe laughed. "Only motherfucker I ever seen no call no show for four days, and not get fired."

"They know they can't find no one to run that machine better than me, for that many hours." I said.

Joe would bitch about his wife and kids for two hours, then tell me it was worth it.

"It's different when you got kids, man" he'd say.

Yeah, different. Different in the same ole fucking Ohio.

14.

Me and the pregnant girlfriend limped along fighting and screaming. She shed a thousand tears, and I proved I was a red blood, blue collar Midwestern American man by shedding none. We took turns screaming the meanest things we could think of at each other. We didn't have any ground rules in place, because we didn't really know each other. We used everything our trauma laced brains could think of as weapons in these verbal wars, and the pregnant girlfriend left back home to her mother twice more before our daughter was born.

I was drunk every day and fighting a war of addiction that I didn't understand and fighting a war of mental illness that I'm still trying to figure out. The pregnant girlfriend knew I was fighting these wars, but she didn't know why.

She was fighting wars of insecurity, and fighting dreams, expectations of motherhood, and depression, and wars of an ever-changing body, flooding with new hormones and chemicals. I knew she was fighting those wars, but like most battle tested crazy addicts, I was too consumed with my own wars to try to help her or understand hers.

Me and the pregnant girlfriend made it to one last doctor's appointment, at the end of a long nine months that took two years off my life.

The doctor said our baby girl was going to come any day now, and the doctor was smiling and the pregnant girlfriend was smiling. I did not smile as I drove us home to pack an overnight bag.

We checked into a Toledo hospital late in the evening, and I sat in a chair next to her hospital bed while we watched strange sitcoms that didn't resemble any reality that I'd ever seen. We watched tv and we didn't talk because we were scared, but we didn't know why we were scared, so we didn't say anything.

Early the next morning the doctor showed up and the war of bringing a baby into the world began.

Watching a baby be born is one of the craziest things that I have ever watched, and I've spent a lifetime watching crazy shit.

There's also a lot of downtime watching a baby be born. Hours go by, growing more pregnant than the next with anxiety, and contractions and pain. Every hour, I'd sneak away from the birthing war room, and walk over to the parking garage to smoke Kool's, and to drink little medicinal drinks out of a bottle of southern comfort that I had smuggled in past the senior citizen security guards.

Late in the evening after the pregnant girlfriend had wrestled with being a mother all day, two doctors and two nurses wheeled her bed into a surgical room, and they spread my pregnant girlfriend's big, soft and warm, naked body, over a stainless-steel slab. They spread her soft warm thighs apart, so we could all stare at my pregnant girlfriend's pussy up close. Her pussy that I had spent a thousand factory hours thinking about exploded into a war scene that was traumatic, and beautiful, and magic.

A baby girl came out headfirst, ripping and tearing my girlfriend's pussy. Stretching it out wide enough to release a football. A baby girl that looked like an alien baby was crying and screaming, and she was covered in half of her mother's blood and guts. I cried just a little, too.

They put the baby girl on my girlfriend's big naked tits. The baby girl stopped crying, and my girlfriend's eyes spilled over like a farm creek in a summer storm. She cried, and I cried, and the baby girl started crying again. My girlfriend that I barely knew wore a soft, make up free face that was so clean, and pure, and beautiful, that I thought that maybe this was love.

15.

I had accrued a week and a day of paid vacation at the factory, so I took a week of it when my daughter was born. By the end of the week, me and the no longer pregnant girlfriend were home in our little one-bedroom apartment with a brand-new baby girl all our own.

I learned to change diapers and wipe a tiny little girl butt with wet napkins. The girlfriend struggled with breast feeding, and her tits hurt.

The baby girl tried to sleep in a baby bassinet next to our bed. She wasn't very good at sleeping for several weeks, so none of us slept much.

That made the factory hours longer and harder, but American Dads aren't supposed to complain about that, so I didn't. I just put my boots on every day, and showed up, and tried to protect my heart from being eaten by the factory machines.

I worked, and showered, and learned how to hold a baby girl in one hand, and a beer in the other.

We took our baby girl to see the Doctor. She was doing ok. The Doctor took the stitches out of my girlfriend's pussy and told us not to fuck for a while. We made an appointment for the next month so the girlfriend could get an I.U.D. put in for birth control.

We made it two weeks before I was climbing on top of her and she was dragging me back inside her. I could tell it hurt her, but she came, and I came, and we were back at the one thing we both knew we were good at: fucking.

The factory hours stacked up and got longer, as weeks of living with a baby girl that wasn't very good at sleeping piled up on me.

One morning I stopped in for two quick beers at the Bucket, after a 12-hour night shift that felt like a week of Mondays. Joe was there, and some others from the factory, and we celebrated me being a dad. I got fucked up drunk on free shots and hand grenade beers and didn't make it home until after noon.

The girlfriend's mom was at our tiny apartment singing antique lullabies to our baby girl. She didn't miss a song note as she stared daggers of death at me.

My girlfriend was napping when I got in the shower, but was awake, and pissed the fuck off when I crawled into our bed, drunk off my ass, and half dead from that week of Mondays.

She whisper-yelled at me for two hours as I drifted in and out of sleep, and slowly faded into headache hangover.

She was tired of being alone with the baby all the time.

What did she want me to do? I had to go to the factory every day.

She thought she had postpartum depression.

I told her to call the fucking doctor.

She wanted me to stop going to the bar.

I told her I wanted a lot of things.

I fell asleep a little. We were quiet a while.

I tried to grab her hips and pull her towards me. Despite all the whispered reminders of my failures, my dick was hard. It was like that at 25.

"You're such a fucking disgusting pig," the girlfriend whisper-yelled.

She was crying a little still, when she took my dick in her lotion soft hand. She stroked me while she whispered in my ear how much she had grown to hate me. It was complicated, but I'm complicated, too. I came in quick ropes on her hand, and on our bed, and on her stomach.

She cleaned us up with a Kleenex and began to whisper assault my character some more. I couldn't keep my eyes open, and I gave up, and drifted away.

There was a 4x6 photograph of me and my girlfriend in a fancy frame on the nightstand by her side of the bed. It was the first photo ever taken of us together. It was after I'd broken my promise to never come back to Ohio. Me and the girlfriend were at a western bar meeting two of her girlfriends, and I was drunk and smiling. She was smiling in the picture, too.

She loved that picture of us.

My eyes opened as glass dust rained down on my naked body.

The bedroom door slammed and it took me about five minutes to figure out that she had smashed that picture against the wall. I was naked and bleeding from a dozen glass dust nicks and cuts, and she was right. I did not care enough to wake up and fight.

16.

In his book *Life*, Keith Richards wrote "For many years I slept on average, twice a week. This means that I have been conscious for at least three lifetimes."

I have thought about that a lot. I'm bipolar, and ADHD and a lot of other things. I've often worked 65 hours a week next to factory machines that live to consume American workers 30 years at a time. The 30-year man fades away to forgotten nothing social security, and the machine stands ready to eat away at the next man that steps up.

I've worked 65 hours a week for so many months and years, that I should be on pace to retire 10 years early, and not always three years behind. But that's not how factory math works.

I've worked so many 65-hour weeks that I've lost faith in the great American Dream that says if you work hard, you will find it.

I was working those hours again, and I had a brand-new baby girl that didn't know how to sleep yet, and I was swinging factory shifts every two weeks. I got upside down, and never knew what day it was, whether the sun was shining, or whether the Bucket was opening or closing.

I worked all day, held a baby girl, fought with, or fucked around with her mother, and I drank. In those old Wild West, untreated bipolar years, drinking was the only thing I did consistently. The second most consistent thing I did was give away tiny pieces of my dreams a factory hour at a time.

I worked, and worked, changed baby girl diapers, drank beer, fought and fucked a woman that hated me half the time. A woman I didn't like as much as I thought I would. I logged beer drunk timeless hours at the Bucket, doing things I wouldn't want my baby daughter to know about, with people I hoped she never met.

I talked shit with Joe at work. We'd started going out to one of our cars on our 30-minute lunch break. We'd drive down the road in front of the factory about three miles to an abandoned gas station that was boarded up. We'd back behind it and park for 10 minutes. I brought the pocket bottle of whiskey. He brought a blunt. We traded medicine for 10 minutes, then we'd drive back careful to the factory.

We'd be at work an hour later, the machines nipping at our dreams and wishes, and our buzzes settling in on us. We'd sneak behind our machines warming our lunches up and eating our soup and sandwiches a bite at a time, in between machine cycle times.

I worked longer, harder hours every day in the factory. I got less sleep, and it was summer in the Midwest. It was hotter than Satan's fury, and more humid than a Florida swamp.

I was changing shifts, and changing diapers, and trying to figure out who I was supposed to be.

I'm bipolar, and when I can't sleep, and when I don't sleep, and when I don't remember to make time to sleep, I will eventually dance with the mania side of my bipolar wars.

Mania is an old friend of mine. I love him and I hate him. He's helped me do things that even I know are impossible, but he's also left me hanging when I've needed him the most.

Mania will only take you so far, but he gets tired, too, and he leaves to sleep. My record is five days dancing with mania before he leaves, kicking away my kickstand, and every time, I crash. I can sleep for two days after a good frantic mania dance.

When the factory calls, and I know the crash is coming, back in those
Wild West, untreated bipolar days, I turned to another friend: powder
cocaine.

17.

In ancient times, ancient man thought that people with mental health problems were being punished by the gods, or under demonic possession.

In the dark ages, the Christians believed that those with mental illnesses needed to be healed by god.

In 1800s America, the mentally insane were locked away in asylums.

In the late 1800s, there was a journalist named Nellie Bly that kept getting in hot water for writing the truth. She finally got pissed because all the newspaper editors kept reminding her she was a woman, and thus not expected to be a journalist of substance. Leave the serious writing to the men, they must have told her.

Nellie Bly invented a new form of investigative journalism, got herself committed to a notorious New York asylum, and survived 10 days in the Madhouse.

Her work exposed conditions of squalor and torture and led to reforms and prestigious awards for her work.

The lock them up in the asylum method of treating mental health, persisted as the most popular method of treatment in America until the late 1950s.

In the late '50s, pharmacies started prescribing pills to combat mental health. The pills are just as effective as the asylum is at confinement.

There are still asylums in use in America. They call them state hospitals.

In modern America, 20% of mentally ill people do not have access to mental healthcare. It is widely believed that an ineffective mental health network in America is a heavy influence on drug abuse, homelessness, gun violence, domestic violence, prison populations, suicide rates, rates of child abuse, and the exponential growth of the popularity of reality TV.

From the beginning of time, until today, the prevailing method mankind has used to deal with mental health, is to ignore it, and hope it goes away.

18.

Me and the girlfriend couldn't sleep because our two-month-old baby girl was learning to sleep finally, but she only slept during the day. Me and the girlfriend couldn't sleep, and I was straight and steady, almost drunk, almost every waking hour.

We were getting edgy and snapping at each other every day. We tried not to yell, because when we yelled our baby daughter cried. The more she cried the more ragged all of us were in the tiny apartment.

We were yelling every day, and fuck-fighting in bed at a level that matched our ever-growing confusion, and chaos and anger.

One day after a long heart chewing night shift and morning long chain drinking dollar beers at the Bucket, I came home drunk, and heart still bleeding a little from the heart chewing I was enduring every day and night. It was getting to the place that I couldn't always stop the heart bleeding before the factory machines rang the bell again. My work boots had holes and were filling up and stinking, from heart blood dripping into my socks every night.

I came home, and the girlfriend was laying in bed naked and stoned. She didn't drink often before I got her pregnant, and even though she was more cool with me using weed to sleep than she was with me swimming in drink all day, she never cared to smoke weed she said.

I asked her where our daughter was. She told me her mom was keeping her, so we could enjoy some alone time. So we did.

We were in bed naked afterwards. I lit a cigarette. She was quiet.

"I still hate that you smoke in the house," she said.

"I know," I said.

"I'm pregnant again," she said.

I couldn't hear anymore. I held her, and she cried, and I was gone.

All hope of ever leaving Ohio came crashing in on me. I held my once again pregnant girlfriend, while the hope in my heart, and the last wish upon a star-daydream vanished forever in a day.

That's the cost of broken, and bruised lovers. I knew it, and so did she.

I crawled back to the factory again that night. Work boots falling apart, and the universe crumbing away. My third night in a row with almost no sleep.

A dawning acceptance smothering me, as I fired up the factory machine. I was going to die in this factory, drunk and old, with a family that was growing bigger by the hour.

19.

All the Midwest factories manufacture misery, and in July, the misery heats up and becomes combustible.

Hot and humid are ideal conditions for growing corn, and selling air conditioners and snow cones, but are not ideal for growing dreams in the factory.

In July, the factory is like a sauna. The air gets thick and humid and chokes you if you take a deep breath.

From the first minute of a 12-hour shift, to the last, every inch of you is covered with sweat. Sweat becomes a second skin. It sits on your legs under your jeans, like another layer of clothing.

White rings form around the necks of your shirts, a salt deposit memorial for all the sweat drops that have travelled through. You put a fresh T shirt on every four hours.

You put medical powder on your nuts every bathroom break, to keep jungles from sprouting in your pubic hair.

You change your socks at lunch. Damp socks in work boots will fuck your feet up. Surviving a deadman's 12-hour shift with a half dozen blisters on the bottom of your once again damp foot is fucking impossible. I've seen a half dozen factory skeletons limp away from the factory and never come back. That's the level of torture.

I've only had to survive it once, but it took six nights of abusing the fuck out of 30 percs I bought in a rusty forgotten smoke shack behind the factory.

The machine breathes fire and steam, and spits cancer dust in your face all day.

The floor fans sit on pedestals and fail to awaken the dead air. The dead fans make cancer dust and machine steam sandstorms.

In July the heat and humidity hammer against you. It sits on your shoulders, and grabs your legs, slowing you down, and tripping you.

The factory makes five-gallon coolers of salt-tab Kool-Aid. It tastes like artificially flavored electrolytes, and they mix it in a big factory sink full of dirty mop water and cancer dust.

The heat and humidity get in your eyes, your nose, and your ears. It fills your lungs. Tries to choke your heart.

In July, in the Midwest, factory hours weigh 3 times as much as regular hours. They make you 3 times as tired as regular hours. Your eyes burn, and sting from drowning in sweat all day.

In July, in the Midwest, the factory hours are 3 times heavier, but the cold beers are 3 times colder, 3 times sweeter.

20.

Halfway between the Bucket and our tiny human storage locker apartment, there was a used bookstore. It sat on a forgotten half street that was still made of brick.

The bookstore was in a long brick building with four storefronts. Its next-door neighbors were a pawn shop and a payday loan business. The fourth storefront housed a dozen start ups before giving it up and staying empty. There's only so much blood you can mine in a poor neighborhood.

The rest of the forgotten half street was residential houses, many split up into four or more apartments.

I lied to myself for months, and said I was going to stop in the used bookstore one day and find some new books to read. I told myself I was going to buy books for my baby daughter, and I was going to read books to my baby daughter.

I didn't know how to be a dad to a baby daughter, but I knew baby daughters should have books, and they should have books read to them. My parents did not read me books. They didn't know how to be parents either.

One day I got tired of not being able to believe anything I told myself anymore, and I stopped in to get some books.

I walked in and stopped, disoriented from a thousand forgotten ghost stories spilling from a thousand forgotten books.

There were books everywhere. Stacked on bookshelves. Stacked on top of bookshelves. Stacked in piles on the floor in front of bookshelves. There were books spilling out of boxes and stacked on top of boxes.

Someone behind a big class counter said "Help ya?"

The big glass counter was full of books. There were books piled on top of it, and next to it, and in front of it. The books were piled so high on the big glass counter that you couldn't see who was behind it til he stood up.

Guy behind the counter was older, but his face didn't tell you that. He was 6' 5" probably, skinny and tall. He had a shiny bald head and a two-foot-long gray wizards' beard, and a large gold cross earring in his left ear.

Told him I was looking for a book for my baby daughter, and he pointed to a book maze in a front corner.

I poked around in a pile of kids books and found one about a starving caterpillar.

I wandered around some poking in book piles, and I found a paperback copy of a James Baldwin novel. It was like finding a smile in a sad week. I read the back cover. It was about growing up in Illinois with a strict stepdad preacher.

I'd read this one book he wrote called *Giovanni's Room*. I read it twice, because it was hard to find new books. I was still holding a personal grudge against America's free libraries. They'd refused me a library card once when I was homeless. Said I could only have a card and could only borrow books if I had a state issued I.D. and a piece of mail verifying correct address.

I tried to explain to the library lady that I hadn't checked my mail in a few years, because there ain't no mailboxes on the street.

She smiled and said she was sorry, but I had to leave now, because I was creating a disturbance.

I tried to explain to the library lady that Andrew Carnegie felt guilty that his fortune had consumed so many American workers, so he built free libraries, and free libraries were for homeless people, too.

She just shook her head. Her plastic smile never wavered, and she called the cops.

I'd been drinking 99 cent tall boys behind a dumpster for three days and couldn't remember what Dickens said in the two tales, and it had seemed important to find out. I looked down and saw that my shirt was ripped, and that I was missing my left shoe.

So, I split before the cops showed up. Fuck Dickens, man, I had to find my fucking prodigal shoe.

People that take showers every day are always afraid of homeless people. You have to stay calm looking and non-threatening, because people that wear clean clothes are quick to call cops.

I had to find my fucking shoe. You can't walk down no sidewalk in America with only one shoe on and not have the cops show up.

I gave up on the library card and stole books when I needed a new friend.

When I read *Giovanni's Room*, I was pissed the fuck off. I knew some gay people that were struggling to be ok being gay, and nobody in high school, when they were fucking struggling the most, had ever bothered to tell us about this James Baldwin guy?

In those Wild West, untreated bi-polar days, I didn't think to look for specific authors in ghost town bookstores. I just poked around looking for smiles in my whiskey-stained heart.

I took the Baldwin book I was happy to find, and the starving caterpillar book I found for my daughter up to the glass counter.

The guy with the wizard's beard said, "o-ho. James Baldwin. That's a good one."

And I said I'd read *Giovanni's Room*. And it had made me think about how hard it might be to be gay in a straight world.

The guy with the wizard's beard came alive under naked light bulbs that could only trickle in light around book piles. The old guy with the face that didn't give away much came alive. His eyes danced with fire that he'd forgotten was hot, and we talked about books for an hour, before he pulled a magic trick and offered me communion from a hip pocket bottle of Jack Daniels.

My new friend told me his name was Lorenzo, and I thought that was a cool fucking name.

He wouldn't take any money for my books when I left three hours later, afternoon bugs warming up their evening orchestra.

"Come back and talk to me about our guy Baldwin again. All I ask," he said.

I drove my rusting to twilight car down the forgotten half street towards home. My eyes stung from no sleep drunks, and lost hopes of second chances.

I couldn't wait to show my daughter the starving caterpillar book.

I hoped when she was older that they never gave her any troubles if she was looking for books down at the free library.

21.

The first time they gave my mother shock treatments, she was at the big hospital 45 miles north on the freeway that went past our small town, but not through it. I was nine. The oldest of her four children, the only one with a different Dad. She didn't remember any of our names for a week.

They still electrocute people's brains in mental hospitals. The theory is, that by triggering a seizure, they can change chemicals in your brain.

They electrocuted my mom's brain over a dozen times during my childhood. Once, when she was locked up at the sanitarium, posing as a State Hospital, 80 miles away in the State Capital, they gave her a series of shock treatments over a 10-day period, and she didn't know who she was for a month.

They lock you up in state hospitals when your only crime is trying to find a way to check out in life. My Mom tried to check out a lot when I was a kid.

I have never had my brain electrocuted. Only bombarded with castrating chemicals, that circumcise your ability to feel emotion, and hang you with erectile dysfunction in your 20s.

Some sanitariums have keypad locks, and they don't give you the codes. When you're crazy, you can't be trusted with access to your own thoughts, or genitals.

If you want to check out, they torture you until you agree to let them put barcodes in your brain.

58

22.

My girlfriend who I had a new baby girl with, was pregnant again. She had a doctor's appointment already set up to get her IUD birth control put in, but we'd fucked around before we were supposed to, and she was sure as fucking-shit, pregnant again.

Me and the once again pregnant girlfriend dropped our baby girl off to the girlfriend's mom, and we went together to see the Doctor who thought she was putting in an IUD today.

I could tell the Doctor was frustrated when the girlfriend told her she was pregnant, and the Doctor gave me a few mean glances, and she gave us both a lecture about how we needed to calm our genitals down some.

The Doctor inspected the girlfriend's pussy, and probed inside it a little, and the girlfriend peed on a stick, and in a cup, and a nurse mined a half dozen vials of blood from her, and looked her all over, in her eyes, and ears, and nose, and mouth with a flashlight.

When the Doctor and nurse were done with the 29-point inspection, the Doctor finally smiled, and hugged the girlfriend, and said, "Congratulations. Outside of needing new tires, everything else looks healthy, and your family is growing. How exciting!" the Doctor said.

It didn't seem exciting at all to me, but the girlfriend was smiling, too, and she looked happy about it.

By the day after that supposed to be the exciting Doctor's visit, me and the pregnant again girlfriend were back to fighting and yelling mean things at each other. The fighting was everyday, because after a year of knowing each other, we had discovered that we didn't like each other much. I was a bum drunk with broken, and shorted wiring inside, and she was tired from learning how to be a mother all day, and she had different wires inside that maybe weren't wired the way they were supposed to be.

But we had a brand-new baby, and we were going to have another one, and we were stuck in a tiny apartment together, the three of us, with a fourth incubating.

I went to work every day, or every night in the factory, depending on which way the hours were swinging. I was using cocaine too much, and I'd started bringing a pocket-sized bottle of cheap whiskey to work in my lunchbox.

I'd wrestle with the machine like that for 12 hours a day. The machine didn't care if I was awake, or a little drunk. The machine ran no matter what, chewing and grinding at my battered heart.

I was stopping at the Bucket every day after work, and I was staying there later, and me and the girlfriend were fighting harder, and louder, and longer every day, when I did make it home.

During one big yell fest, she threw a beer bottle at me, and I ducked, and it smashed against the wall, and she threw another one, so I picked up the big square TV and I smashed it on the living room floor, and she stopped throwing beer bottles, and she got our brand-new baby girl, and she left back to her mom's again.

I told her I was happy to see her go, because all she ever did was nag the fuck out of me for drinking, and bitch at me for not being home enough, and I called her names I'm not proud of having called her.

She was gone for a few days, and I was pissed about it, and I stayed at the Bucket for long, four-beers-an-hour shifts, and I worked longer shifts at the factory.

One night while the girlfriend was still gone to her mothers with our baby girl. I was in the middle of a long grinding shift at the factory, and I hadn't slept in days. The Mormon boss, and his boss walked past my machine, and saw me behind it. I'd stacked some plastic empty parts totes together to make a chair, and I'd sat and fallen asleep behind my machine.

The Mormon boss' boss was yelling with spit flying everywhere by the time I woke up, and by the time he was done yelling 15 minutes later, all the other machines had stopped, and the operators I worked with stood gawking at us.

I didn't say nothing back to the Mormon boss' boss. I just stood there and took it, with my insides burning away in rage, and my oil pressure gauge struggling to contain it all, without letting me blow my top.

I was pissed all night, and at the end of my shift I had to go to the factory HR department, where the Mormon boss' boss gave me another scathing lecture, this time accompanied by the tired ass HR rep, and they wrote me up for sleeping. The HR rep made a big deal telling me that the write up would stay in my permanent employee file, and if I was caught sleeping again, they would fire me.

I went down to the Bucket, and started drinking dollar beers, and $2 shots. My inside wires were sparking and arcing, with anxiety from no sleep, and too much cocaine and whiskey. My heart was drunk, and full of anger, about how everything was fucking hopeless. Girlfriend and baby gone, every day all day in the factory, and still falling a little farther behind every week.

There was this guy that was at the Bucket a lot, and he was tall, and too fat. He spoke too loudly, and he shared too many strong opinions all the time, and he knew something about everything. This guy always got on my nerves at the Bucket, but lots of people get on my nerves.

He was there that morning, and someone had brought up the couple year old war in Afghanistan, and the tall, too fat, too loud motherfucker started in on how we should just nuke the fuck out of them dirty ass desert dwellers in the Middle East, and how we should take their oil and use it for America.

"No more A-rabs, and unlimited oil. Perfect fucking world almost right there," the motherfucker said.

There was a lot of hatred in America towards the Middle East, then. There's always been a hatred that I've never understood, but the hatred was stronger in those early, post 9/11 years.

I was drinking dollar beers, and $2 shots, and my insides were jumpy, and full of an angry fire that was burning me inside out.

I started thinking about people that lived in the Middle East. I knew they didn't drink alcohol there, because of religion. I'd read about it in a book, once. But the men there had to have jobs, just like we all had jobs, right? There had to be dads there with new baby girls, that were working every day, and trying to learn to be a dad, right?

I said something about Afghanistan being full of everyday people, that were just trying to take care of their families probably, and how they hadn't done anything to deserve to be nuked.

The tall, too fat, too loud, know-it-all laughed like I was a fucking comedian telling the best jokes, and he called me a pussy for sticking up for them dirty desert people.

The tall, too fat motherfucker had been getting on my nerves for a long goddamn time, and I was edgy, and burned out. My internal oil pressure gauge had been whistling warnings of a popped top for days, and I didn't know til then, but I was looking for a reason to explode.

I told the tall, loud motherfucker that his mother was a whore, and I was getting bored with fucking her all the time, but just because he'd called me a pussy, I was going to go to her house tonight, and I was going to fuck her in the ass.

He jumped off his barstool, and I jumped off mine, and everybody in the Bucket was yelling and screaming. The motherfucker was six inches taller, and 80 pounds heavier than me, and he was pissed because I'd insulted his mother.

But my heart held more hurt than most men, and I'd been angry since the day I was born.

He threw punches and I threw punches, and we fell to the floor, wrestling, and punching, and scratching. He got a finger in my eyeball and tried to poke my eye out, and the oil pressure gauge popped loose, and I exploded.

I was punching and punching when three or four guys got me off the loud fucker, and I punched at them some more, but they got me away from the motherfucker and out the door of the Bucket.

I went home and drank some more in silence. The TV was still sitting in a pile of plastic, and glass splinters, with TV guts lying all over. I didn't bother with the $10, dollar store clock radio. I just sat, and drank until I passed out in the chair, and when I woke up my face hurt.

I looked in the mirror, and I was banged up a little. The eye the motherfucker tried to poke out was purple, and swollen, but not shut. A black eye and a bloody lip ain't nothing but superficial shit, so I washed my face, and put my boots on, and went back to the factory.

23.

The girlfriend came back after a week, and she helped me clean up the broken TV, and the beer bottle glass that was all over everywhere.

She asked about the black eye that was just a dull gray now, and I told her. I asked about her mother and her father, and she told me.

We took the baby daughter to the store with us, and we bought a new TV. And we went back to our everyday hopeless lives.

She stayed home and learned how to be a mother in the tiny apartment, and I escaped to the factory, and to the Bucket, who had let me back in their door after a week suspension for the fight. The loud motherfucker didn't come around anymore.

I was stopping at the used bookstore on the brick half-street once every week or two, to see my friend Lorenzo the wizard, and to buy books for my baby daughter, and sometimes I was buying books for myself. I read a book to my baby daughter everyday that I saw her. She liked Curious George books, and I did, too.

I started reading books to myself again. When I was home, and the girlfriend was watching the new TV, I'd sit and read books and drink beer, and our baby daughter would lie on her belly on a blanket on the floor.

I'd been at the bookstore a half dozen times, when one time I bought a John Steinbeck book for me, and a different Curious George book for my daughter.

Lorenzo charged down a Steinbeck rant, and I jogged behind him trying to keep up. We talked about *East of Eden,* and *Grapes of Wrath,* and of *Mice and Men.*

I hadn't known anyone that knew who John Steinbeck was for three years.

Lorenzo told me that he'd escaped to Canada to avoid being eaten by the Vietnam War machine. Said he'd come back home but he couldn't escape the war inside of him. Said you can't run away to asylum from yourself no matter how queer you are inside. Said he came home and finished his degree. Got a job teaching high school dropouts and juvenile delinquents how to read blueprints at a state funded tech school for deviants.

Lorenzo the book wizard told me he'd always wanted to be a poet. Said he'd spent too many years in Canada trying not to get eaten by war. Said his parents didn't believe in being queer. He said they don't put your name on black granite plaques when you're a casualty in family holy wars.

Back at the tiny human storage container apartment, the once again pregnant girlfriend and I had started in with the arguing and fighting. She was getting bigger, and meaner the more weeks she was pregnant, and I was the same mean most of the time, and the same drunk.

24.

I'd been at the factory, swinging shifts, and wrestling with the machines for over a year now. I'd gotten another raise, and I was making almost $16 an hour, and I was working all the hours they would let me, and I was still behind all the time on our bills, and shit.

Me and the once again pregnant girlfriend found an old, small two-bedroom house to rent, and we moved into it with our baby daughter who finally got her own bedroom.

We bought a crib at the Goodwill thrift store, and I put it together in my baby daughter's new bedroom, and I bought a little bookshelf for all her books.

The house was old and small, and it didn't have a shower, just an old claw foot bathtub. There was a tiny back yard, and a garage off a dirty alley that had ripped up trash bags and trash all up and down it. It wasn't much, but the rent was cheap and it was close to the factory, and close to the Bucket.

The girlfriend was getting bigger, and me and her had started talking about going down to the courthouse to get married.

I'd been married already, and that hadn't gone so well, but I had a baby now, and another coming soon, and when you have babies with someone, you marry them. That's what you do in Midwest America.

I didn't want to get married, but didn't see any other way around it much, and the getting bigger pregnant girlfriend was talking about it all the time. She wanted to get married she said. She wanted to have my last name, the same last name as her daughter, and she wanted us to be a family. I said we were already a family, and last names didn't really mean much, but if it's what she wanted, we'd do it, and we did.

I put my nice Levi's on, and a button up church-shirt, and she wore a pink maternity dress that her and her mom picked out, and her mom and dad and our baby all went to the courthouse with us, and we bought a marriage license, and a preacher man that loitered around the courthouse married us in a stairwell for $40 cash.

We didn't have wedding rings because we couldn't afford them, but we had a set on lay-a-way at K-mart. We all went to dinner at Bob Evan's after, and my new mother-in-law and my new father-in-law congratulated us both.

They kept our daughter overnight, and I took a vacation day from the factory, and me and my new wife that was pregnant with our second baby, drove up and stayed the night in a fancy hotel in Detroit. We did the same things in the fancy hotel that we would have done at home, except I got drunk off a bunch of mini whiskey bottles that cost me $130 when we checked out the next morning.

I went to the factory every day, and got my heart chewed on, and I got drunk at the Bucket, and my wife was bitching at me about my drinking all the time, and she was yelling louder and louder about how I was never home.

Turns out she had expected that since we were married, and now that I was a dad and a husband, that I would start acting right. I told her that a marriage license was just a piece of paper, and that it was unreasonable to expect that piece of paper to change a man. Besides, I worked every day, and sure, we were behind on bills all the time, but she didn't have to work, and her and our daughter had most everything they needed. What the fuck was there to bitch about?

We fought longer and harder again every day, and we didn't fuck nearly as much as we had just months ago. One day in the middle of a pretty good fight, I brought that up, and that really set her off.

She yelled that all I ever wanted was a whore that cooked and cleaned, and I said what's wrong with that, and our daughter was lying on a blanket in the middle of the living room crying and screaming because we were fighting.

We yelled some mean things, and she started throwing picture frames at me, I called her names, and the baby was screaming and crying.

The wife got a knife from the kitchen, and I grabbed her wrist, and got it away from her before she stabbed me, she kneed me in the balls, and before I could hit her she took off out the front door, running down the sidewalk in nothing but a t shirt and panties.

I took off after her, she was pregnant, but I was faster, and I got her in the middle of the next block and I grabbed her. She was crying and screaming with snot bubbles all over her face. There were neighbors coming out on their porches to see what was going on, and I grabbed my wife's arm and yanked her back towards our own block.

She started hitting me with her other hand and I let go of her wrist to block the punches and she started yelling, and screaming, and cussing, and punching me as fast as she could with both hands. I grabbed her up in a bear hug so she couldn't punch.

I was yelling about how we had an audience now, but that it didn't matter. I said are you trying to get me to hit you? Are you happy with the scene you've created? I snatched her off the ground and tried to carry her home, but she was still kicking her legs, and yelling and cussing, and we almost made it back to our house when the cops rolled up, and this time the motherfuckers took me to jail.

25.

I stayed the night in jail, went to court in the morning, and was back home to an empty house. The baby's room was empty. The wife's soaps and shampoos and toothbrush were gone.

We had lasted for three weeks as husband and wife.

I went back to the factory and back to the machine. I'd missed a day of work because of jail and court, and I endured another threat of firing because of it.

I was getting pissed about the threats. Fuck this motherfucking factory. There's a dozen more like it down the street.

But I kept showing up, and letting the machine chip away at my heart, and any dreams and aspirations that might still be left in there.

I drank at the Bucket with Joe and hung out with Lorenzo at the bookstore. Lorenzo knew more books than all my schoolteachers in my small cornfed hometown. Lorenzo loved whiskey, and I did, too.

The wife was still gone after a week of factory shifts, and Bucket shifts. I called her, and her mom answered and told me to fuck off. I called again a few more times, til finally my wife told me to fuck off, too.

There was a woman I knew that hung out around the Bucket sometimes. She was in her late 30s but looked older in daylight. She had an office job somewhere, but everyone knew she was addicted to pills, and that if you gave her pills or money she would let you fuck her.

So I bought her some pills one night from this guy I knew in the factory that sold them out of his lunchbox, and the woman went home with me, and she stayed with me for a few days, and I'd go to the factory and grind the machine, buy some pills, and go home and fuck her.

On the tenth day, me and the woman took some pills, and drank and fucked. We listened to the radio all day. I'd bought a decent radio at the pawn shop next to Lorenzo's wizard bookstore, and me and the pill freak woman drank and fucked some more and listened to the radio.

On the 10th day, my pregnant wife came back home with my baby daughter, and her mom was with her. They found me passed out, drunk and stoned and naked, in bed with a woman in the same condition.

It was chaos. The wife was throwing shit at the woman as she was trying to grab her clothes, and the mother-in-law was yelling, and the baby was crying. The woman and the pregnant wife were fighting on the ground pulling hair and scratching eyes. The pill freak woman was still naked, and I got them separated, and the wife started hitting me with a shoe. I was still naked, too.

The mother-in-law was yelling, and the baby was screaming, and I got the shoe away from the wife, as the woman ran out the front door, and got away, carrying her jeans and underwear under her arm.

There was screaming and yelling, and a baby crying. The radio kept playing classic rock. The bedroom window was open, and the curtains danced slow in the breeze.

The wife threatened to get a knife, and we yelled some more. The father-in-law showed up, and him and the mother-in-law took the baby back home with them and left me and the wife to fight it out.

So we did.

We fought and yelled and said all the mean things we could think of until it was midnight. The wife was in a big pregnant heap lying on the bed crying. The radio still played classic rock. It was a good radio.

My pregnant wife said she'd went to the doctor and found out we were having another baby girl. All she wanted to do was come home and tell me.

And I told her she had told me to fuck off and hadn't talked to me in two weeks.

She said you didn't even come to see your daughter for two weeks.

I said I had to work every day to pay all our bills.

She said it didn't take you long to find a fucking whore, did it?

And I reminded her that she had told me to fuck off and hadn't talked to me for two weeks.

And I stopped arguing, and we finally fell asleep for two hours, before I had to get up and put my work boots on and go back to the factory.

26.

The native people around the Amazon rain forest have been chewing the leaves of the coca plant for thousands of years. It gives them energy.

The Catholic Church came to South America, and they tried to ban the coca leaf.

In the mid 1800's a German scientist discovered how to make cocaine from the coca leaf, and Sigmund Freud got addicted to it. Then he invented psychology.

Doctors tried to use cocaine for anesthesia, and they killed people with overdoses.

Entrepreneurs put it in their products and sold their products as get-well tonics.

In 1914, America banned cocaine, the coca leaf, and opiates, and they blamed it on the African Americans, even though almost all the cocaine use in America was by middle class white people.

In the 1980s humans learned to cook cocaine and turn it into crack rocks. Crack ran through America like a modern pandemic does, and America once again blamed it on the African Americans. Ronald Reagan declared a war on crack and locked up thousands of African Americans. Crack surged more than ever.

In the 1980s, cops started the Drug Abuse Resistance Education (D.A.R.E) program to teach kids the dangers of drugs. It was ineffective, but it took them 30 years to figure that out.

There are some credible suggestions that a former American president worked with the CIA to bring cocaine in bulk on airplanes to his state when he was governor. That former president was white.

Today, the illegal cocaine industry in the United States is worth over $30 billion annually. Coca Cola is still made from a coca leaf. There's a factory that extracts the cocaine and sells that to a pharmaceutical company. They still use cocaine as an anesthetic for some surgeries.

No one knows if our government is still at war with drugs. They've been fighting the war on drugs for 50 years. If the war is still on, news headlines say they're getting their asses kicked.

Cocaine is one of the most addictive drugs on the street. Crack is far more addictive than powder cocaine.

I have loved powder cocaine like a lover. More than I have loved my physical lovers. I like crack, too. And I've done a lot of other drugs, but cocaine was always my favorite.

27.

My pregnant wife was batshit crazy this pregnancy. That's not a professional diagnosis, and I'm not talking shit about her.

She got depressed and wouldn't take a bath or do anything around the house. Then she started picking fights with me every day, and night.

We hadn't fucked much in months, and not much since the other woman was here. We got in a big fight every day. Our baby daughter was crawling now, so we kept her in a play pen when we were fighting, and she screamed and cried every day, the whole time we fought.

Jesus, this is no life for a baby.

One night when the pregnant wife had thrown everything in her reach at me, she ran to the kitchen for a knife, again. I bear hugged her so she couldn't grab one, and she struggled against me.

I let her go. Said maybe if you still gave me them blow jobs like you used to, maybe I'd come home more.

She got pissed and we fought some more, and I said fuck it and left and went to the Bucket.

The woman that liked pills was there, and I got a $2 shot and a mason jar draft beer. There were a few dozen people in the Bucket. Some at tables, some at the bar, and some hustlers shooting pool on the dirty faced pool table.

I drank my shot and went and played some songs on the jukebox that wouldn't stop yawning.

I sat with the woman for a bit. She kissed me hello, and I bought her a drink. She drank patron and coke, and I drank beer and did coke. After a bit I told the woman that I had some pills hidden in a baggie in my glove box. Said I'd hoped I would see her here today.

We went back to her place. She lived in a small rusty trailer in a small, rusty trailer park. Her trailer was dirty, but it wasn't filthy. We took the pills, and we went back in her rusty bedroom, and made friends for a little while.

28.

The first time I did cocaine, I was 19 years old, and I was at a party that featured two strippers. It was a big party, and there were a lot of drugs. I saw people doing lines of coke off one of the strippers' stomachs, and I took a number. When my appointment came around, the coke was moving south. I did what everyone else was doing, and I did coke off the smooth shaved skin of a stripper, the skin right above her pussy.

The first time I did cocaine, I loved it so much that I bought some, and took it home. I bought more, days later. Then more. Then more.

Cocaine is like all the good things in life. The more you do it, the more you want to do it. Then its effectiveness wears off, because you're doing it all the time, so you have to start doing more and more coke to feel good.

When I was 20, I got arrested for depositing bad checks. They were my checks from my checking account. I was writing them out to myself, and depositing them in money machines all over town, and they said I owed the bank $2k.

That was my first war with cocaine. It ended in jail.

There were more wars. Some had casualties, some didn't. Some of the wars cost me jobs and friendships. Some wars cost me everything I had. Some ended in rehab, more ended in jail.

I have loved cocaine, even though my addiction to cocaine has cost me everything at least three times in my life.

I haven't used cocaine for over 17 years. Sometimes still, late on a Friday night at a casino poker game, when my bar drink of choice, Red Bull and Cranberry juice, ain't getting the job done...I can still taste cocaine in the back of my throat on those late nights. I'll close my eyes sometimes, and I can remember the burn. The numb. The rush.

I close my eyes, and I can see lightening spread through my veins, racing through arteries, jolting a chewed up, blue collar heart to life.

Then I open my eyes. I'm still middle-aged, and tired from two lifetimes of factory hours, and a lifetime more to go.

29.

The pregnant wife ran off back home to her mother's again. Took our baby daughter with her.

She came back, then took off again.

It got so I didn't know if I was married half the time anymore. I didn't know if we still lived together.

I put in shifts at the factory, drank at the Bucket, hung out with Lorenzo at the bookstore and at the Bucket, and hung out with Joe at the Bucket, and sometimes at the bookstore, and once in a while, I'd stop over to see the woman that liked pills.

I was only home a few times a week.

My wife and I made it to the hospital together, and I prepared myself to witness my second birthing war.

I was drunk all day while my wife battled the labor process. I was out in the parking garage getting another cigarette, drinking rotgut cheap whiskey, when they moved my wife into the birthing room.

When I got back upstairs they got me sanitized and I put on a hospital robe, a hair net, and gloves. I looked like a blue snowman.

I got in the birthing war room just as my second daughter came into the world. I was standing around watching everything go down, and it was time to cut the baby's umbilical cord. I was supposed to cut it, but

I didn't. The Doctor did.

There was blood and guts, tears and stitches, but everything went like it was supposed to.

Later, after our baby was getting checked over, and my wife was back resting in her own hospital room, the Doctor stopped me in the hall.

She asked how much I'd had to drink today. I told her only a little because I was always nervous about babies being born.

"You smell like a distillery," she said.

But she didn't say anything else. And our daughter was healthy, and back in with my wife.

30.

I took a week of vacation from the factory when my second daughter was born. The wife and the baby came home after a couple of days, and my mother-in-law was over at our house helping a lot.

I didn't like my mother-in-law, and she didn't like me. She was my second mother-in-law. The second mother to watch in horror as her daughter fell into love, or what was supposed to be love, with a crazy motherfucker like me.

Both of those mothers in law did the same thing. They bitched and nagged at their daughters, to try to get me to either act ok, or to get them to leave me.

A few days after my second daughter was born, and before I went back to work, my father-in-law, mother-in-law, and wife, staged a half assed intervention for me.

I had an advantage at the intervention. This was their first one, but it was my 50th.

50 interventions is an estimate. I don't know the exact number.

My wife cried. Said she couldn't live like this. My father-in-law said he wanted me to be a good father. My mother-in-law said she didn't want her granddaughters raised by a heathen.

My family hadn't been around my adult years enough to care about how much I drank, but there had been others that were around, and they did care.

By the time I was 25, the following people had tried to talk to me about my drinking: multiple girlfriends, a wife, a wife's family, cops, coworkers, employers, employee assistance program reps from various factories, more cops, lawyers, judges, rehab counselors at rehabs, other patients in those rehabs, friends, various bartenders, other barflies, a cousin, an uncle, and one janitor at a highway rest stop. The janitor had found me passed out by the dumpster corral when he was emptying trash.

All those interventions had the same results, and this one wasn't going to be any different.

I listened, then told them I didn't drink any more, or any less than I did when they'd met me. I said I drink. It's what I do.

It's not that I didn't know that I was an alcoholic. I did know. And it's not that I didn't want to drink a little less. I had tried to drink less for a handful of years. I tried only drinking at home. I tried not using drugs. I tried to only drink after 5pm. I tried to only drink a 6-pack a night. I tried to only have two drinks a night. I tried to only drink on weekends. I tried not drinking before work. I tried not drinking at work. I tried not drinking on an empty stomach.

The wife cried some more. Told me to think about the future of our daughters.

I said our daughters had diapers, and food and formula. They had clothes. They had books and a roof over their heads. They had everything they needed.

No matter we were six weeks behind in the rent, and I hadn't paid the light bill yet. It was only two or three weeks late.

The mother-in-law begged me to not drink, but I'd heard enough. I left and went to the Bucket.

I went back to work after the week off, and everything went back to normal. Or normal as we knew it.

A few weeks after that, my oldest daughter turned one. We had a birthday party. My brother-in-law and sister-in-law were up from Dayton to celebrate with the family.

And a few weeks after that, my oldest daughter took her first steps while I was at work in the factory.

31.

According to the Bible, mankind has been using alcohol to get drunk, and fucked up, since Old Testament times. There's a wild story in the Old Testament about a major prophet getting shit-faced and trying to show his dick to his daughters.

According to scientists, who don't ask us to have faith, mankind has been using alcohol to get fucked up since before we were mankind. They believe our more primitive ancestors were drinking before they dropped out of the trees and walked upright.

In 1920 the United States congress made a constitutional amendment banning the sale, production, or transportation of alcohol. They called it Prohibition.

One of the biggest groups fighting for the ban of alcohol was a large organization of Christian women. They were mad that their husbands were spending so much time in saloons, and not enough time at home.

Prohibition didn't stop alcohol. The mob and the mafia stepped in and took up the job of providing alcohol to America's drinkers. They created speakeasies, underground and illegal taverns and bars. They say that New York City had upwards of 100,000 illegal speakeasies operating at any given time. And that was just New York City.

If you lived in a small town that only had organized crime in the city government, and if your town didn't have a speakeasy, you could get a prescription from your doctor to buy medicinal alcohol at the local pharmacy.

In 1933, the United States Congress passed a new constitutional amendment repealing the Prohibition amendment.

The Busch Beer company delivered a case of Budweiser to the White House in 1933 to celebrate. They used Clydesdale horses, and a big wagon.

Having nothing else to do, after busting Al Capone, and with alcohol legal, the Bureau of Prohibition changed their name to the Bureau of Alcohol, Tobacco, and Firearms.

Alcoholics Anonymous formed in 1935 as a nonprofit altruistic way for alcoholics to find help. AA claims that alcoholism is a disease, and the only successful treatment is complete abstinence. No word on how much influence the women's temperance movement had on AA's stance, if any. The Women's Temperance Movement is still in existence today. Some women never let go.

Mothers Against Drunk Driving formed to try to convince Americans to stop getting fucking hammered and getting in crashes and killing children. Drunk crash fatalities were cut in half, then almost in half, again. Mothers are still against Drunk Drivers.

The U.S. drinking age is 21 years. You can serve in the military for three years before you can legally drink a beer in America.

Sales of legal alcohol in America tops over $250 billion a year.

Clydesdale horses, and a beer wagon are still used by Budweiser for promotional purposes in parades and multi-million-dollar Super Bowl Ads.

Alcoholics Anonymous has around 1.3 million U.S. members, and claims new members have a 27% chance of staying sober for one year.

32.

We had a three-day holiday weekend from the factory. Only the Monday holiday was paid, and we were losing a lot of money not working overtime on the weekend, but the factory said the machines needed a break so that they could get massages from the maintenance men whose full-time jobs were to stand around all night in case the machines needed a quick massage.

My chewed-up heart needed a break, and Joe said hell yeah. He needed a break, too.

Me and Joe went to the Bucket after our last shift that holiday weekend. I drank $1 mason jar beers, and he drank out of a can. We had a bunch of $2 shots, toasting days off, and being away from the factory that turned American dreams into more money for Wall Street.

Me and Joe both liked to get fucked up, so we did. I had a bunch of coke, and he had a bunch of pills, and we started mixing those in between rounds of shots.

About noon, Joe says, "Hey, let's drive over to the titty bar and look at pussies." Seemed like a good idea, so we did. I drove, and Joe had a blunt, so we smoked it on the ride over and I was feeling pretty fucking good.

The Strip Club was half empty in the afternoon. It was dark as midnight inside, except for purple and pink neon lights dancing around a stage up front.

Me and Joe ordered a bucket of beers, cashed in some $20 bills for some $1's.

We sat at the dollar trail around the stage and watched a 30-year-old naked woman with zombie eyes slide down a shiny pole. She swung her legs open in front of us and showed us all of her secrets.

The Strip Club smelled like sweet whore perfume and pussy, and I loved it.

There was a shot girl with a big round tray of test tube shots of liquor. The shot girl was topless, and she stood with her tits looking me in the eyes. Me and Joe bought some test tube shots and we got some for the shot girl, too.

The shot girl put her tray down and sat in my lap. She kissed my neck and whispered in my ear. Her breath was warm, and her whispers were wet with lust.

Me and Joe told the shot girl we had some coke and pills, and she took my hand and put it inside her panties so that I could play with her pussy, and we shared our coke. We drank test tube shots, and we had a dozen of the best secrets in Toledo rubbed on our faces in private dances. We were fucked up, covered with glitter and whore perfume, my face smelled like pussy. This might be heaven.

The Strip Club was packed because it was night all of a sudden. One stripper was licking another stripper's secrets right in front us, and Joe let out a country boy holler and everything was pussy, and drugs and laughing hearts.

"Let's drive up to Detroit to the casino," Joe says, and that seemed the best idea of the day, so we did.

I drove up I-75 north, and Joe rolled another blunt. We got to the casino and they had free liquor for big gamblers, and me and Joe told them we were, so we drank for free, and free liquor goes down fast and smooth.

I don't remember when we left the casino. I don't remember anything after drinking free liquor at the casino.

I woke up two days later in a dark motel room. The lamp was knocked over and broken. The TV was on but it wasn't telling American stories. Everyone was speaking in Spanish. Joe was passed out on the floor under a little desk. He had a pair of black lace panties stretched over his almost bald head. He was naked, and snoring like a motherfucker.

We were in a lowlife motel in Detroit. And we didn't know why or how we'd gotten there.

My two-bedroom tiny house was empty when I got back home. I was broke and had a hangover that felt like a lifetime of sin was jumping on me all at once. My heart was broke and nearly dead.

33.

The first time I had to talk to a counselor, I was eight years old and in the third grade.

The kids were playing kickball at recess. I liked playing kickball because I was good at kickball. Better than most of the other kids.

David Jenkins said I couldn't play kickball no more. He said I stuttered, and the kids had heard my mother had tried to kill herself, and that I was maybe a retard, and they didn't want to play kickball with me. Said I might be a crazy retard like my mom and they didn't want to catch it.

I told David Jenkins that I hoped his mom got killed, and he threw the rubber kick ball from five feet away and hit me in the face.

I got so mad I couldn't see, and me and David Jenkins started punching each other. The teacher kicked us in the ass and chased us all the way to the principal's office.

Our principal had a full beard that could never hide all his big shiny teeth.

David Jenkins was scared, and he lied to the principal. He said we were just playing Mr. Principal. We didn't mean nothing.

I told Mr. Principal that if I got a chance, I was going to smash David Jenkins' face in for making fun of my mom for trying to kill herself.

Mr. Principal made me see the school counselor. She was a real old lady, and her office smelled like it had housed old ladies forever. I was eight years old, and she told me that eight-year-old boys weren't supposed to say they were going to smash people's faces in.

I told her I understood, and she said if I promised not to say I would smash people's faces in, then I wouldn't have to come talk to her no more, and she probably wouldn't have to make me talk to the cops.

I promised.

A month later, I was in the hallway at school, and I saw David Jenkins bent over taking a drink out of the water fountain. I shoved his head down, his mouth hit the fountain's water spigot, his blood ran down his chin, and ruined his sweatshirt.

I had to see the old lady school counselor every week for a while after that.

34.

My wife would only come over to the tiny house with our two tiny daughters a few evenings a week. She wouldn't move back home because she said if she did, she was going to stab me in the neck with a butcher knife while I was sleeping.

She brought our tiny daughters over in the evenings, and I would buy a pizza or some fast-food burgers. I'd drink beers and read Curious George books to my daughters.

My wife who said she couldn't live with me, said the only time she thought I was human was when I was reading books to our baby girls.

She said of course I couldn't even be human for once without drinking.

My wife didn't want to fuck much anymore. Said I was disgusting. Said she was depressed. She'd gained 80 pounds with back-to-back babies, and she didn't like her body.

I said her mouth still worked just fine, and she chucked a half full beer bottle across the room and made our daughters cry.

I told her I was tired of her shit. I said I get it. I'm a piece of shit. I'm fucked up and not human. But I don't never make the babies cry.

She told me I made everyone that ever tried to love me cry.

I told her I hated her.

She told me good. Said she wished she had never met me.

I was tired from a lifetime of deadman factory shifts behind me, and two lifetimes still to go.

My baby daughters were crying. My wife that hated me and didn't want to be my wife was yelling, and I screamed. They all stopped.

I kissed the girls and walked out the door and went down to the Bucket.

35.

I had to go to court for the time the cops saw me wrestling in the front yard with my wife. The cops said I was disturbing the peace. They said I was intoxicated in public, and they said I had resisted arrest. These were all misdemeanor things, these things the cops said I did.

I had a public defender. He was 55 and looked like he had spent all his years in the same frumpy suit, wandering the halls of the Toledo courthouse, in scuffed brown shoes that needed a face lift.

The public defender did a good job getting me out of trouble. I had to go to anger management class, and counseling, then pay a fine, and all the trouble would go away.

I had to go to court on my court date and tell the judge I'd done the things the cops said I did and tell him I agreed to go to counseling.

I put my good Levi's on, and a nice button up church shirt, and I drove downtown to the five-story, city court in downtown Toledo. The court building was typical 1970's architecture; ugly concrete and glass.

I sat in a big court room with a hundred other Toledo Citizens that had been accused of doing misdemeanor things.

In America, judges think they're god. This Judge in this courtroom was no different.

Some court assistant with a big stack of manila folders yelled a name. The person that belonged to that name went up front, through a little half-door, to a table in front of the judge.

The Judge told the person to tuck their shirt into their pants. Judge said this is my court room and you must look presentable.

The guy in front of the Judge looked confused. He was wearing a hooded sweatshirt.

The Judge yelled, tuck your shirt in, and the guy started trying to tuck his hoodie into his sweatpants.

All morning, the Judge that thought he was god yelled at people. Say yes sir in my courtroom. Say no sir. No talking in gallery. He charged three people with contempt and sentenced them to a month in jail for not following his commandments.

It was three hours of this before the assistant with the folders said my name. I went up front and my public defender came over to the table with me. He'd been having coffee and doughnuts over with the prosecutors all morning.

I already had my church shirt tucked into my Levi's, so the God-Judge didn't have anything to bitch about. That seemed to annoy him.

We all said our lines as scripted, and when it was official the God-Judge moved on to make more commandments. The guy after me wore a sweater, and it was not tucked.

I managed to fit my anger classes into the middle of my heart chewing factory shifts. It was the third time in 10 years I'd taken anger classes, and I passed the classes with ease. I knew the right things to do and say.

I went to the counseling sessions, and the therapist said I was a little crazy so she gave me some Prozac.

The Prozac made me feel numb inside, but I guess that was supposed to be better than feeling like it was raining glass shards and bumble bees in my heart all the time.

I went to the factory and stood up to the machine day after day, night after night.

Joe told me I seemed calmer with the Prozac.

I told him I didn't feel anything at all.

The wife came back home with our two baby daughters. She bitched, and nagged. Our baby daughters cried, and shit in their diapers.

Wife constant nagging. Babies crying and shitting. Machines growling and barking. Jukebox singing and yawning. Beer drinkers laughing and crying.

It was all noise in the background. I was plastic inside. Everything was gray. There was no sun. There was no moon. No smile. No frown. No up. No down.

The wife said this is the best stretch of husbanding and fathering that you've ever had. She said she could never love me. She said, but maybe she didn't hate me as much as she thought she did.

We had a cookout in the tiny back yard of our tiny two-bedroom house. My wife bought me a $40 kettle style charcoal grill, a spatula, tongs, and two-tine fork set for grilling. She bought them for me on Father's Day. They had a major university's logo on their handles.

My father-in-law and I drank two beers each, while we watched charcoal slow, and meat heat. He said he loved watching my oldest daughter walk around so much. Said she climbed on their dining table last week and ate half a chocolate cake with her bare hands.

We laughed about that.

"What a mess," he said.

He said my youngest daughter was making the funniest faces.

We laughed about that.

We ate off paper plates. Some potato salad from the grocery store. Some potato chips to go with the meat.

My mother-in-law smiled at me. Said she was glad to see me home every day. Not starting no shit or nothing. She didn't stare one death glare at me all evening.

Me and the wife stood on the porch holding our girls in our arms, all four of us waving goodbye to the grandparents. The grandparents were smiling big whole Midwestern smiles, big happy, warm heart smiles.

The wife and I put the baby girls to bed, each in their own cribs in the room they shared. They each had their own little bookshelf, with their own little libraries.

The wife brought me a beer, and we sat on the sofa together. We turned on the TV, like everyone else in America. I put my arm around her and wondered when the sun would rise again. The gray is exhausting.

The wife went down on me. Right there on the sofa. And I could only get half hard, and it took me 27 minutes to get off. I know. I watched the fake cuckoo clock in the dining room the whole time.

Even a willing and eager blow job didn't feel like sunshine anymore. This was supposed to be the happiest moment of my life. Prozac hid all the ghosts that danced in my midnights, sure. But it also smothered all the sunshine that sometimes could leak into my rusting heart.

If this was the best happy that I could be, than it was over for me. If this was it, then I was done.

I put my boots on the next morning. Carried my lunch box into the factory. Let the machine grind away at me.

12 more factory hours on the odometer of my heart, and it was already a thousand miles past due for a tune-up.

36.

Selective serotonin reuptake inhibitors (SSRI's) are the most common form of treatment for depression. Prozac is an SSRI.

SSRIs were first used to treat depression in the late 1970s.

In 1987, Eli Lilly Pharmaceutical Company finally got around to marketing Prozac 10 years after they'd received their patent for the drug.

Prozac quickly became the best-selling drug of all time.

Prozac, and other SSRIs are most commonly prescribed to treat depression, although most major studies say that the risk of side effects outweigh the benefits of taking the drugs.

SSRIs are also prescribed to treat dozens of ailments including, but not limited to, anxiety disorders, manic depression, bipolar disorder, eating disorders, PTSD, chronic pain, obsessive-compulsive disorder, and addiction to reality TV.

Most major studies say there isn't any conclusive evidence that SSRIs provide any benefit in the treatment of any of the ailments it's prescribed to treat.

The most widely reported side effect of SSRI's is sexual dysfunction. Studies report the drugs affect 40-98% of those that take SSRI's, at different levels of sexual frustration. Almost every single prescribed patient of an SSRI has experienced at least a mild, negative effect on their sex life.

A negative effect on one's sex life is one of the most common reasons people stop taking their antidepressants.

More than half of those prescribed SSRIs report having negative sex life consequences long after they stop taking the pills.

Another of the most common side effects of taking SSRIs is an increased chance of suicidal ideation. Reports say you're 80% more likely to have thoughts of killing yourself if you take SSRIs. You are 130% more likely to report an increase in hostility and agitation.

European health agencies have recommended only prescribing SSRIs to treat the most severe depression cases and long-term moderate depression cases that have proved resistant to other treatment. They suggest the negative side effects are too great to prescribe your average depressed patient.

They say at any given time, one in five Americans is taking a prescribed SSRI.

I have been prescribed five different SSRIs in my adult life. None of them proved to have any long-term benefit. All five of them caused an increase in my already broken suicide ideation monitor that sits busted on my brain's control board. All five of them caused increases in my hostility and agitation.

That is my personal experience. I cannot suggest a course of action for you.

I've grown to wonder if mental health treatments aren't a little like religion: it all depends on what you choose to put your faith in. Religion seems to work for millions of people. Yet, atheism is on the rise.

Taking pills must work for millions. Yet, hundreds of thousands have the reverse testimony.

Major studies say placebo pills, fake pills, are effective more than half the time.

37.

I was drinking from a half empty bottle of Black Velvet whiskey with Lorenzo and Joe one weekday afternoon.

The bottle of Black Velvet was half empty, and so was everything else.

Lorenzo had rescued a stray kitten that had the good fortune of meowing outside the right store front on a forgotten half street. The pawn shop next door would have sold the scrawny kitten. The payday loan place would have given it away as a door prize to people too poor to care they're being charged 700% interest.

Lorenzo had a 13-year-old cat at home, and the old man cat didn't like the young kid cat, so Lorenzo brought a litter box to the bookstore and the kitten was now a bookstore cat. He called the kitten Doc, because when it meowed it kept forgetting the 'me' part and walked around saying ow, ow, owwww, so Lorenzo called him Doc.

Doc was napping on a waist high pile of books by the front door, and Joe was passing the Black Velvet back around.

"I been on the pills a lot," Lorenzo said. "Never liked them. Needed them sometimes to get through."

"I can't feel the warmth of the sun anymore, man," I said.

"You been quiet as fuck a lot bro," Joe said. "Like you're thinking or something."

"I don't think," I said. "Just breathe, and move around. Work. Sleep. Drink."

"Yeah. It gets like that'" Joe said.

"I can't do it," I said.

"I couldn't either. Only for as long as I had to," Lorenzo said.

We finished the bottle of Black Velvet. Joe had a blunt. We all three went in the back room to smoke it. Lorenzo turned a sign on the door to say out to lunch.

We sat on some rickety ragtag mismatched chairs in the back room. Lorenzo had a bunch of bookshelves in the back room that were full of fuck books. The kind of novels with naked art on the cover, full of typos, and full of x-rated fucking.

There was a bunch of old *Playboys* and *Hustlers* for sale. And a ton of hardcore, full HD color fuck mags that catered to more flavours of fucking than I could dream up.

I liked to go through the fuck novels. I couldn't believe there were this many stories about this many flavours of fuck.

We passed the blunt in the back room, surrounded by hardcore porn literature.

"Lots of people got arrested for this shit," Lorenzo always said. Every time we smoked one. Which was almost every time I visited.

Lorenzo got reminiscent in the afternoons if he drank too much in the morning, and got high in the afternoon, he would talk a lot, when he got stoned.

"I was taking Prozac when I was dating the gay bar owner." Lorenzo said. Marijuana clouds floating above our whiskey drunk heads.

"He kind of liked it. I couldn't never get off." He got his and didn't have to worry about mine much.

The blunt went around.

"What happened to the gay bar owner?" Joe asked.
 Lorenzo smiled an almost closed eye lid high as fuck smile.

"He didn't come home for a week once after a big queen bitch fight. He'd sleep in his office above the bar sometimes."

"He came home one morning and this young twink I'd picked up the night before was just leaving."

Lorenzo hit the blunt and passed.

We were quiet for a passed round of the almost too short to smoke blunt.

"Gay bar owner says who cares you crazy pervert. I've been fucking my new bartender for months."

Lorenzo had a fresh pocket bottle of Jack.

"A couple rounds," I said. "I gotta get home."

"Me too," Joe said. "I gotta 50-minute drive."

"You should move closer to town," I said.

"Fuck that," Joe said. "Too many people."

We drank Jack.

"I told the gay bar owner I knew he'd been fucking bartenders for a long time." Lorenzo said.

"Why didn't you say nothing he asked me," Lorenzo said.

"Well, I used to like you," I told him.

And we all laughed.

I went home with new books for baby girls.

I stopped taking my Prozac.

38.

They say that stopping an SSRI prescription cold turkey is dangerous. The risk of suicide goes up, and the risk of withdrawal symptoms and a relapse of depression are concerns.

One of the most common reasons mental health patients give for abruptly stopping their medication is the feeling that they're better, and no longer need the medication.

I have never stopped taking pills because they made me feel so good that I felt I didn't need them. I have always stopped taking psych meds because of negative side effects.

I've had weird headaches from some. Had a loss of appetite, or an increase in appetite. I've had nausea and confusion. I've often had increased suicidal ideation, and agitation. Some pills have made me more aggressive, and some made me not give a fuck about anything. Some made me want to watch reality television.

Most of the antidepressants I've been prescribed have tried to smother the bright colors that live inside me. Most have, at some point, squeezed out the sunshine and the smiles that live in my fading factory heart.

I was good off the Prozac for a week. I had trouble sleeping right away, but I've always had trouble sleeping.

I made it a week before me and the wife had an argument. It wasn't a bad argument even, just a garden variety one. But it was the first we'd had in a minute.

Then I got tired because I hadn't slept much in a week, so I got into the cocaine for the first time in a while, and I was balls to the wall getting my heart chewed on every day.

I was getting hammered at the bucket every day. The cocaine, and unregulated bipolar heart were conspiring to drink in volume. I was using cocaine and whiskey-soaked tourniquets to try and stop my heart from bleeding so damn much.

Joe's youngest kid was sick, and the doctors didn't know why, and Joe was worried, but he was a Midwestern blue collar dad, and he couldn't show he was worried, so he used some different, but same, tourniquets.

My wife and I got into another, bigger fight. The baby girls were screaming, and my head felt like it was buzzing with a thousand dying mayflies.

The cocaine and lack of sleep sparked a bout of mania, and I went full tilt, kick shit and take names alpha male.

I had to be restrained twice from my dick is bigger barroom fist fights in my second week.

By the third week off the Prozac, me and the wife were back to debating who hated who more and were slinging threats of divorce and death like they were handfuls of candy flying off a parade float.

Joe's kid was getting sicker all the time, but the doctors still couldn't figure out what was wrong, so Joe's kid was in the hospital, and Joe took off work to take turns on guard duty, staying the night in the hospital with his kid.

Lorenzo seemed more agitated and paranoid than usual, and even Doc the cat that had adopted the bookstore as his home wasn't concerned much with getting his ears scratched.

Everyone was a little off, and the world seemed tilted funny on its axis. Maybe Mercury was retrograding, or the sun was shedding its skin and sending solar flares spraying into the ozone like 4th of July grand finale fireworks.

My wife and I were lobbing hand grenade insults at each other every day. Then she got the cannons out, and was laying a volley of explosive death threats, and I called in the air support from my fighter jets and dropped the big bomb.

All you were good for was fucking and keeping a bed warm, I told her.

She said I was a shit tornado that had roared through her normal American life and covered everyone around me in my own shit.

I put my work boots on and crawled back to the factory machine. Some dude named Greg was forced in from another swing shift to cover Joe's machine.

Greg was short and bald and had no chin. He had logos from arena rock bands tattooed on his forearms, and when I asked about them he said he'd gotten the tattoos as a young man, before his kids were born, back when he still had a life all his own. Greg liked to walk all the way down to the main break room and watch TV on his breaks, and I was left to chain smoke cigarettes and nip the bottle of Jack by myself. I was left to endure the heart chewing of the machine all on my own.

One day after I'd been awake for three days, working factory shifts, drinking in volume at the Bucket and at home, me and the wife got in a big fight, and she told me she was leaving and taking our daughters with her. You're never going to see them again, she said.

I told her to go fuck herself because she was worthless and no one else would want to fuck her anyway, and she left with the girls. I told her I hated Ohio and that it was her fault that I was fucking trapped here, in Midwestern purgatory hell.

By the time the sun set on another broke man's 12-hour factory shift, my wife and her parents had moved everything that was hers or my daughter's out of the tiny old two-bedroom house.

All I had left was our banged-up discount warehouse queen bed and a half decent pawn shop radio.

What more could a broke dick factory man want?

39.

A lot of jobs in a lot of factories aren't the most physically demanding jobs. Sure, the factory is hot as balls in the summer, and colder than the heart of a republican governor in the winter.

The thing that makes factory jobs impossible for those that can't hack it, is the endurance of the job. You'll show up at the factory the same time every day. Park your car in the same spot of the factory parking lot. Walk the same steps in the same work boots, to the same machine every day.

You'll work and sweat in the summer, changing T shirts and socks. You'll do the same job, over and over, making the same motions, over and over and over again, until you can do the motions without thinking about it. You can do this job in your sleep.

And you WILL do this job in your sleep. You'll do the same job, the same way, a thousand times a night, until the motions of the job become such a part of who you are that you will do the motions in your dreams.

You'll stand on factory concrete in work boots designed for safety over comfort. Hour by hour, week by month by year, you'll stand on factory concrete. Factory jobs plant seeds of arthritis in your knees, and the seeds are watered by the everyday beat down of boot on concrete, and the arthritis grows a little more each year.

Your legs will sprout varicose veins like blood rivers trapped just under skin. Your hips will break down. Hip socket grinding bone on bone. Your spine will twist and discs will bulge.

You'll stand next to machines that spit cancer dust in your eyes all day, and if you have a family, you will spend more time making memories with the cancer machine than you will with that family.

You will spend hours and hours next to your factory brothers and sisters. You'll know their quirks, their character flaws, and how they take their coffee within a matter of months.

You'll take breaks at the same time every day.

You'll rush to the bathroom, drain your bladder, wash your hands, rush to the place designated for smokers. Years ago, there were smoking break rooms inside most every factory. Now, you're lucky to find a smoke shack outside a side door.

You'll chain smoke two cigarettes, making jokes with dirty, bone-tired coworkers, then rush back in, 15-minute break is over. Time to fire up the machine again.

You'll eat your meals on the same breaks at the same time schedule every day. Watch a time lapse of four seasons fast forward, as you walk the same steps in, and the same steps out every day, year after year.

There is a weird, never talked about anxiety, born of this living the same exact day most days of a man's life.

The American factory worker is expected to do this for 30 years, and often more. Day after day. Boot on concrete grinding knees, and dreams of freedom to dust.

Factory shifts are designed to maximize factory output, and not to accommodate the needs of a family.

Factory shifts are designed to maximize profits for Wall Street portfolios, not to accommodate social lives, hobbies, and community events.

You'll miss out on important family events. Have to take vacation days to celebrate birthdays and anniversaries.

If a family member dies, you'll get three days, or five days, to bury them, and you'll be back singing my-fucking-knees are killing me, on this goddamned concrete-floor-blues, trying to think of anything but your dead loved one.

This endurance of factory life is impossible for many. More than half of all Americans walk into a factory at some point in their working lives. They'll push up their sleeves, lace their work boots tight, and wrestle with cancer breathing machines. Day after exact same motherfucking day, week after week, and sometimes it's a year in, sometimes eight years, as many as 20 or more for a few, but the endurance will break their will, and they'll leave and never come back.

The HR office pulls another application out of a pile in the drawer. The next man up, shows up in new work boots bright as sunshine. The machine stands ready to rumble, ready to chew on fresh heart.

The factory is a marathon of living the same day, the same way every year, until you're too old to stand for 12 hours. Go park up front of the factory next time shift lets out. See how the old-timers all wobble. All lean to the left? Limp, and twist, one shoulder higher than the other, hair gray and steel battered hands with fingers in permanent claw from years of holding the same part the same way for so long that their hands stand on permanent stand by, ready to wrestle with the machine.

The factory isn't for everyone. The factory isn't for anyone. No eight-year-old American kid dreams of growing up to work in a factory. American kids dream of being celebrities. Or firemen. Or astronauts, writers, cowboys, dancers, athletes, singers, or actors. And maybe some of them will live their dreams.

For the rest of us, those that can't find anywhere else to plant our childhood dreams, there's the factory and its heart chewing machines, standing ready to give us a paycheck to keep on getting by til we can figure out what it is we want to be before we die.

40.

In many ways, I have the ideal traits of an American factory worker.

I'm a college drop out with a high school diploma. I don't have any skilled trades licenses, or technical training. I'm smart, and don't mind working hard hours and long hours. I've worked in almost all the kinds of plants and factories you'll find in the Midwest, and I've ran almost all the kinds of machines they have in those factories.

I walked into my first factory at 18 years old and learned to run three story tall printing presses that could print 30,000 magazine booklets every hour. I later ran smaller, single sheet printing presses, in a smaller and more depressed factory.

I've made fire-retardant hood pads for pick-up trucks, on giant machines, and learned that I was allergic to fiberglass. I'd go home and take three cold showers a night and drink myself stupid trying not to dig the flesh off my arms. It was like living with a million pieces of tiny glass growing in your skin.

I moved on to make plastic bottles, a thousand of them an hour, for well known laundry soap companies. Then I drove a forklift at a steel wire place. Then drove a forklift at a warehouse, then another. Got certified to teach forklift-Hilo instruction and safety classes.

I built transmission parts on an assembly line for a bit, then got a good job as a maintenance man, monitoring, maintaining, cleaning and repairing all the hydraulic tanks in a big machine shop. Paid good, and I got to sit around and nip whiskey and read books while on the clock a lot.

Left that job for a woman that lived in another state. Including the mother of my two daughters, I'd done that for three different women in three separate states. It never went well any of the three times.

I worked in a plant that milled paper from trees. You couldn't smoke on the property there. Boss said if the paper mill caught fire it would burn for a hundred years. We all smoked on the property anyway. Some of us got caught and got fired for it. After nine months, I was one of them.

Got hired in a factory that assembled metal file cabinets.

I worked for a few years in a glass factory that had five story tall furnaces that ran 24/7, 365 days a year. A furnace that big took 90 days to heat back up and get flowing. The giant cancer breathing furnaces ran at several thousand degrees Fahrenheit, literally melting sand into glass. It was 400 degrees up close to those furnaces. You had to wear special space man suits to work on them. The special gloves looked like the gloves a medieval knight would wear and weighed two pounds apiece at the start of your shift, and 20 pounds apiece 12 hours later. All of us furnace operators got lazy about the gloves and space helmets. All of us had no eyebrows, and no hair on our arms. They couldn't shut down the furnaces for Santa Claus, the Easter Bunny, Labor Day parades or Thanksgiving turkeys. So whole generations of glass making families have gone their whole lives incomplete at the holidays.

I worked for a while in a concrete plant. Then in a plant that made those giant ass concrete tunnels you see construction crews burying under roads and shit. We made 240 of those concrete pipes every day, Monday through Saturday. They were on little railroad tracks so we could line them up to bake in a giant oven all night while we slept. We smoked cigarettes while we worked in that plant. I smoked two packs of Kool Milds every day. One pack at work in the factory, one pack after in the bar. Not the Bucket, but one very similar. I worked with a Filipino-American man there. He was older, probably early 50s. He was a Vietnam veteran for the American Marine Corps, but all his killer brothers suspected he was sympathetic with the Vietnamese because he looked like them.

I used to eat my bologna sandwich lunch with him on our lunch breaks because he told the most insane fucking stories. He was one of the most perverse humans I've known, and in all these factories you can imagine the perverts and weirdos I've run across.

My Filipino friend's name was Angelo, but most of the tobacco chewing roughnecks in the plant called him assholio. They thought he was Chinese. He never corrected them.

"It doesn't matter," Angelo said. "They don't know where the fuck China is, either."

Angelo told the most insane dirty jokes with a perfect poker face. If he got a good reaction out of you for a crazy bad joke, he'd laugh and laugh, his 5'6" 120 body coughing and laughing till he couldn't breathe.

Angelo had a cigarette lit at all times. He smoked Pall Malls, three packs every factory shift. He drank as much as I did after work in the almost Bucket. Me and Angelo worked side by side in the hot oven all day, pushing the 600-pound concrete pipes into straight lines and locking their 400 lb wire cages shut around each one. It was hard, physical work all day. Angelo did it with a cigarette hanging out of his mouth and a long sleeve loose flannel shirt. We'd drink Jack together at lunch and be half drunk in the oven, wrestling 600-pound concrete pipes. He never broke a sweat. I was twice his size in bulk and strong from living a heavy life, and he kept pace with me, telling dirty, fucked up jokes the whole time.

Angelo told me once that no matter how many Vietnamese he killed, Americans never accepted him as one of their own.

"I was born in California. The most American place. Where all the American Dreams live," he said.

Angelo was twice my age. He had kids my age. The three of them had college degrees and careers in other cities. They called on Father's Day. Came to see him and Mom on holidays. Angelo told me he doesn't think America accepts his kids either. Two of them are doctors. The other an Ivy League grad.

I worked 12 hours a day, six days a week, for 15 months with Angelo. Went to two holidays at his house with his family. Drank a hundred gallons of Jack Daniels with him.

The roughnecks started calling me a Chink lover and saying me and Angelo were fags. Angelo ignored them. I did too, for a while.

Until one night at the almost Bucket, one of them asked me what it was like butt fucking a Chinaman every day. It was the day after Veteran's Day. Angelo earned two Purple Heart ribbons in Vietnam and gave away his ability to find sunshine in his dreams. Said when he closed his eyes he only saw death, and he knew what it looked like, and what death smelled like. You can never forget the smell of burning flesh. The sound of ghost shrieks of humans burning alive. They poured fire on our own people, man. Angelo told me you could smell the barbecued human flesh in the humid jungle air for weeks, until the rains came and even the typhoons and monsoons couldn't wash my friend Angelo's sins away.

These rude ass motherfuckers didn't even know he was born in California. Or that his father was a hero in World War II. That the guy they called assholio was a real-life American war hero. It was the day after Veterans Day, the day after I'd asked my friend Angelo about what Vietnam was like. And he had told me the things that I'm telling you now.

I saw Angelo's jaw tighten shut, the only sign he had heard the roughneck's stupid jokes. It was all it took for me. I couldn't take it no more. I smashed a half-full of beer mason jar over the roughneck's head. After three minutes of fighting off six men trying to break up the fight, the roughneck went to the emergency room, and I went looking for a new job.

I'm not a bad ass. There were different results in many bar room brawls to come. And there were other factory brothers and sisters that lit fires in the dead chambers of my human heart, like Angelo had, over the years, but none taught me about stoicism like Angelo did. None taught me to grow a gut of concrete to protect your heart from the American machine and the American cancers of racism and ignorance. Angelo gave me a copy of the *Meditations of Marcus Aurelius.* I still have it. And still learn from it.

I moved on to a parts staging warehouse for an auto plant, then to a steel plant in a good maintenance job in a fucked-up factory. Then to a middle-class union job, that has almost given me hope of rising above poverty.

I've worked all over the Midwest, for temporary companies and good union jobs, and all the factories in between. I had the good traits of good fodder and fertilizer for the factory machines that grow money for Wall Street.

But I've never been able to take the same growl from the same machine for long. At 25, I couldn't keep the same woman, the same address, the same zip code, same state abbreviation in postal address, same job in a factory, same haircut, same favorite author, same brand of beer, or same brand of rotting through my guts liquor, I couldn't keep the same goddamned anything for more than a year or two, at best, and there were always a lot of 30 day wonders in between the year or two's 30 day lovers and 30 day factories.

41.

I got fired in the factory one midnight.

Joe was still off work. The Doctor's knew what was wrong with his youngest child, now. It was cancer. His kid was back in the hospital every three days for aggressive cancer treatments, and Joe's Mom was helping plan a potluck benefit at a country church for Joe's kid. Joe and I had okay insurance at the Factory, but the deductible was a few grand and American factory workers do not get paid time off for the Family Medical Leave Act, a law Bill Clinton signed, that says the factory must give you time off so you can take your eight-year-old kid to Midwestern university hospitals for poison cancer treatments, but the factory does not have to pay you for that time. So Joe was falling behind, even with his just getting by side job-drug hustle.

Lorenzo met a young guy named Tristan. Tristan was my age, young enough to be Lorenzo's son. Tristan wore pink T shirts that showed his perfect hairless belly button and worked at a local record store.

Tristan was so fucking cute, I wondered why I stayed straight. Guess maybe I was born this way. Didn't stop Tristan from flirting with me.

Lorenzo was in hot lust love. I guess that kind of love is about the same for most of us no matter what we do with our genitals, or with whom.

The tiny two-bedroom house sat empty except for that high mileage queen mattress, the decent pawn shop radio, and a reliable coffee pot that cost me $12 at a Kroger's grocery store. Music, a bed, a way to make coffee, a way to keep beer and cake cold, and a way to heat beans and rice is all a man needs to get by in life. Maybe a notebook and a decent $2 ink pen in case he has a wayward thought. Maybe a good book or two as friends on an empty heart, whiskey drunk night.

The two-bedroom tiny house was empty like that, with just get by stuff, for weeks. Decent enough music on the decent radio. In between lots of capitalist commercials. The big local rock station was almost 50/50 during working hours, with give us your paycheck schemes and decent rock n roll music that was getting a little less decent every decade.

The rice and beans got me by, and my beer was cold, with my store-bought chocolate cake in the fridge. Always had a sweet tooth.

But my dick was hard a lot because I was off the Prozac, and because a half dozen therapists have said I was hypersexual, and half of them said it was because of trauma endured, and studies now say, maybe trauma stored in my DNA, passed down from one broken generation to the next. No, Hank Williams. The circle will not the fuck be broken. It's trapped inside the cells and chromosomes that live inside us. The cells that make us who we are. That build us from baby to casket.

My house and heart were empty, save for classic country night on the local country channel. They were calling it Cash Wednesdays. Playing a Johnny Cash song every 30 minutes all night on Wednesday nights. Felt good to feel some blue-collar hymns of hope and heart, from the best poets of past generations.

My heart was empty. I hadn't seen my daughters, or my supposed to be wife in weeks. No one answered my phone calls. My father-in-law called the cops once when I tried to stop over to visit. He said I was drunk. I said so what. You're ugly. My mother-in-law screamed mean things at me in a high soprano opera voice. My baby girls stood watching and crying in a front window of their grandparent's house while their mommy and daddy talked to a bunch of cops with a bunch of cop cars in their grandparents' front yard.

I stayed away. After four weeks some court papers came in the mail. They said my wife was asking for child support. I got drunk and listened to almost decent rock n roll. Went to the factory and walked the same steps, walked the same motions all day, 12 hours.

A week after those papers, and some more court papers came by signature only mail, and they said my wife didn't want to be my wife anymore. She didn't have money. I knew this. She hadn't worked in two years. I ain't mad or being mean about it. But I started cashing my paychecks at the carry out for $5 a week, because I didn't trust our joint bank account no more.

She had almost middle-class parents, who could almost afford a good attorney for their daughter who needed to divorce her crazy alcoholic husband and move on with her life. The headlines of our life often write themselves, but it's only those willing to read the full story that understand.

All I had was a factory job that I couldn't stand anymore, and a weekly overtime paycheck that almost lasted til the next check, next week.

I hadn't fucked in three months because my wife hated me and left me, and my friend that I liked to do pills with was busy doing pills with another friend of hers in her rusting trailer.

I was at work in front of the machine one midnight. Joe was still off work. Lorenzo was still consumed with chasing ass, or cock, or whatever chasing him and Tristan did.

None of it was their fault. Maybe it was the affect of two months off Prozac. Maybe it was loneliness, anxiety, and alcoholism.

My head was buzzing that night. It wasn't a headache. Just a buzz. I was hyper aware of everything all night like I'd done some powder, but I hadn't done any in a few days.

I heard every growl, clunk, and snarl of all the dozen machines around me.

I was raw, and ragged feeling from long drunken hours and short nights with no sleep. My heart felt like cicadas were waking up from a 17-year nap.

The Mormon boss and the big boss stopped by my machine, just as

I ran out of fresh parts to feed it. I had just lit a cigarette and leaned against the now idle machine.

The big boss was in a pissy mood.

"You're only supposed to smoke on break time." He said.

"I know," I said. "But we can smoke here by the machine on break. And usually no one cares."

"Why is your machine not growling and spitting cancer dust in your eyes," he said.

I was irritated. My head was buzzing like a dozen of those bald monks that all hum Buddhist words together.

The big boss could see the empty parts rack behind me.

The big boss knew that forklift Bob was forever falling asleep on his forklift and taking illegal naps. Forklift Bob had been there 40 years and wouldn't quit. The factory was all he had.

The big boss was fucking with me and there wasn't any reason to fuck with me, except he was the big boss and he could do it.

My head buzzed like a big highway paving machine rumbling to life and I was sick of the shit in this factory. I couldn't stand it one more fucking minute.

"My machine can't keep up, I'm working so fast tonight," I started in on him.

My numbers were solid. And I knew it. It's why forklift Bob was behind.

"Pfft. Yeah. That's why we're three weeks behind in production," he laughed.

"We're three weeks behind because you're working us all to fucking death, and you motherfuckers won't hire any more workers," I said.

116

The big boss was mad now. Forklift Bob was pulling up with fresh food for the machine. He stopped to listen.

The big boss yelled at me. "If this job is too much for you, leave and go somewhere else. You should have been cleaning your machine while you were waiting for parts. I'm writing you up."

"You ain't writing up shit, Jack," I said. "You can go fuck yourself," I said. I was already moving to grab my lunch box.

"Fuck you. You're fired. You're fired," The big boss yelled.

The Mormon boss stood there like a deer lost in the headlights and about to be eaten by the machine.

I grabbed my lunch box and swung around and hit the big boss by accident with my lunch box. He started yowling that I had assaulted him and he had his walkie-talkie off his belt and was screaming for security guard back up on the wrong channel of the radio. He was still on the production channel and not on the emergency channel.

I yelled that if he didn't stop whining and screaming like a bitch I was going to stomp the shit out of him.

My head buzzed all the way out the factory gate. I didn't bother to run my timecard through the time clock one last time.

Just walked away, the machines in the factory all silent, and machine and man gawking at something fucking different for once.

Security rolled out to the parking lot on an electric golf cart with police lights just as I was pulling out of this same factory one last time.

42.

When I walked out of the factory, I drove home to the tiny two bedroom, almost empty house.

I got an old Merriam-Webster's dictionary out and opened it. There was an envelope inside with about $500. It was cash left in my pocket after long bar crawls and stashed away for another stormy day. Or for a divorce attorney. Whichever came first.

I wanted to take that $500, put some of it in my gas tank, and drive away from Ohio, until I found somewhere that felt better. I wanted to get the fuck out. Go somewhere else. But I didn't.

I hadn't fucked in three months, so I took some money from the envelope and went looking for a friend.

I drove down 2am inner city streets until I found a working woman. They call these women sex workers now, and they've called them a lot of things over the years. It didn't matter to me. I loved them.

When everything else was complicated, the whores were simple. You told them what you wanted, they told you how much, and you did it. Nothing else mattered except getting a little fucked up and fucking.

The whores never cared much about the politics of love and sex. They only cared about drugs and money, and they used the last currency they had to get those things.

I found a 2am working woman. I wanted to get some rock, but she preferred smack, so we got some.

We laid on my rusty but trusty queen bed and got set up and got right.

We listened to music and we fucked and it was good. We lay around some more and fucked some more. Harder now, rougher, more serious.

We got set up again with the little smack left and got right.

The working woman left back to the streets in the morning. I stayed in bed and drank cheap whiskey and did not care about much of anything.

A few days later, Joe took a break from the hospital visits with his kid, and we stopped over at the bookstore to drink with Lorenzo.

Tristan was there and we had a bottle of Jack.

"At the Bucket, they said you knocked down the big boss?" Joe said.

"Nah man. I bumped him with my lunch bucket. That's all," I said.

"Ha. What did the big boss do?" Joe said.

"Screamed for security like a bitch," I said.

"Security walked you out?" Joe said.

"Nah. They didn't show up on their cop-golf cart til I was pulling out," I said.

"Fuck that place anyway," Joe said, even though he was technically employed there. He needed the health insurance now, more than ever.

"What're you gonna do?" Lorenzo said.

"Find another factory and get my heart chewed on there," I said.

"You could stud yourself out," Tristan said with a wink.

Tristan was wearing black lipstick and black eye shadow and a black see-through fish net shirt.

"Nah. I don't think that's for me, Tristan," I said.

"You'd be surprised about how many old queens that'll pay good money for you to fuck them," Tristan said, and blew me a silent kiss.

"I imagine I would be surprised, but there'll be a factory hiring somewhere," I said.

Joe was laughing now. Lorenzo was, too.

"All you gotta do is change jerseys once in a while," Joe said between laughing wheezes. "Be a team player," Joe said.

"If this is all it takes to get you to switch teams, I'd have signed up sooner," Lorenzo said. He was laughing, and wheezing, too.

"Fuck all you guys," I said.

And Tristan said, "For how much Daddy?" And that was it. We all laughed and drank Jack the rest of the afternoon.

43.

I stopped in a neighborhood corner store, bought a 6-pack of tall boys, some smokes, and a newspaper.

Newspapers then weren't newspapers now. Back then, the newspaper was still printed every day, and over half of America still read it.

Back then newspapers had a help wanted section in the classified ads every day, and if you were looking for a job, that's where you looked.

I went home and turned on the radio. It was a classic rock day in between all the commercials for used cars, furniture stores offering no interest for a year if you had qualifying credit, and banks offering home loans and free checking accounts.

I cracked a beer and read through the paper. Cracked another beer and dug into the help wanted ads.

There wasn't fuck shit out there. Some fast-food jobs, a couple temporary staffing companies, hiring for peanuts and no benefits, and two sales jobs.

I once had a sales job as a younger man. I wore a shirt and tie and shaved my face every day. I was pretty good at sales, but I hated every minute of it. I've never been good at lying for no good reason, and you can take this to your bank with your free checking account: if a company has to pay someone to talk you into buying their shit, there's some bullshit in the deal somewhere, somehow.

Since I quit that sales job, I've done a pretty good job at not wearing shirts and ties, and I haven't shaved my face but a handful of times.

I got tired of all the commercials, and the evening DJ talked too much, and played too much newer shit. So I turned the radio off and went down to the Bucket.

It was busy. Dinner time or happy hour in dive bars, where happy people drink their dinner.

I ordered a buck and a half mason jar draft beer and stood at the end corner of the bar. It's where I always sat or stood. There's a lot of dive bars in America where everyone knows your name. *Cheers* ain't got a market on that shit. Real dive bars ain't that bright inside. And their story lines are real and far more complicated.

There were about eight regulars at the Bucket and we all had our general area around the bar. Mine was at the end, back by the pool table and jukebox.

Angie was bartending. She worked a lot of week-night evenings because her old-man was an over-the-road trucker, and he was usually only home on the weekends.

Angie was 40, probably 5'6" and 180 lbs, all ass and tits, and she was biracial. Half black, half Mexican. She never had kids and I don't know why.

I had a thing for Angie and she knew it. She cock-teased me like a motherfucker about it.

She was 15 years older than me and married. But she liked to dry hump me over by the pool table at least once a week, slow dancing with me to love songs playing on a jukebox that kept falling asleep all the time.

Angie was my friend and being friends with a woman wasn't something I was ever too good at. It's a complicated thing listening with two heads and thinking with two heads all the time.

Somehow, despite her bouncing that big ass up against me at least once a week, we hadn't fucked, and that was as honorable a thing as I had done in a long while. Best to hang on to that as long as I could.

Angie came around the bar and gave me a hug and a kiss. It wasn't a friend hug and a kiss, but it wasn't quite the hug and a kiss of lovers meeting for the third time. It was somewhere in between those two things, and that was enough to get both my heads thinking.

"Hey. You know I'm single now," I told her.

She was back behind the bar washing her hands.

"No you ain't. You're just separated," she said.

She was pouring two mason jar drafts at the same time.

"I got fucking papers and everything," I said.

She was back with a fresh hand-grenade draft beer and a shot of Jack.

"But not papers to fuck me," she said, leaning in and blowing me a slow kiss.

She was wearing a Bob Marley T shirt with a four-inch V that she'd ripped in the front with rusty bar scissors, so when she leaned in you could see her tits bounce in against each other and splash back two inches into place.

I've always been an ass guy. I've traded too many paychecks to admit chasing women with big asses. They still visit me, with sweet smelling perfume, in my mid-afternoon, middle-aged-nap dreams. But watching Angie's tits jiggle when she leaned in was worth all the extra tips she got, plus a lot more.

After the happy hour dinner drinkers went home and things slowed to just a handful of long-haul drinkers, Angie poured herself a beer and put some songs on the jukebox. She didn't play any love songs though. She played some sad ones.

Angie came and sat on a barstool next to me where I was standing on the end.

Angie's husband was an over-the-road trucker, and he had a girlfriend in Iowa. He drove out to Iowa on his route, picked her up, and she lived over the road with him in his sleeper semi for three days a week.

He told Angie about it, and Angie had a boyfriend for a while. A young white dude that sold pills. Damon was an alright guy. He still stopped in the Bucket once in a while, and I bought pills from him sometimes. But Damon's baby mama found out about Angie. Damon had four kids with her, and she found out he was fucking Angie. Me and another regular had to carry Damon's baby mama out of the Bucket one night when she came up there to whoop Angie's ass.

Angie said she was too old to fight young bitches over their baby daddies, so she mostly stopped fucking Damon. But sad people need pills, and they need to fuck. It's how you prove your worth when you have nothing else.

Angie told me some sad things about still sort of loving her husband and how she felt like a sad bar joke, with everyone knowing her husband had a girlfriend.

"Maybe I should have gone out on the road with him," she said. "He asked me to."

"Maybe," I said.

I wasn't too good at giving advice on how to deal with the sad. I used pills, liquor, and chasing ass, but I was smart enough not to brag about it.

"I hate road trips," she said.

"Yeah. Doesn't seem like that would have worked either," I said.

My beer was gone. Angie's beer was gone.

She turned on her barstool so that I was standing between her legs and we were face to face.

"You wore this shirt because I told you it made your blue eyes pop, didn't you?" She said.

She rubbed her hand over the crotch of my Levi's and laughed, moving off the barstool and was a step away from me before I could react to her grabbing my junk.

I smacked her on the ass hard and she yelped. Her ass was big, but it was solid.

She brought me another beer and a shot, then went to refill the drinks of the thirsty long-haul drinkers.

Angie came back over, staying on the business side of the bar. She had another beer.

She made some honey-syrup jokes about being a bad girl and needing a good spanking because she knew I liked those jokes.

I was drunk and if I stayed around tonight, I was in trouble.

I'd been at the Bucket for about six hours, but it didn't feel like it. Six hours never feels like six hours at home.

That's the thing about dive bars that *Cheers* didn't understand. The regulars are orphaned travelers waiting at bus stop-dive bars, just waiting out their time. Waiting for the next round. The next lover. The next town.

Home is where they let you back in, no matter how many times you've been orphaned and divorced.

44.

It went like that for a few days. None of the factories around town seemed to need any fresh fodder for their machines. The help wanted ads were like one of those speed dating events they host for those that have been left behind when the marriage train rolled through. You drink a lot of champagne punch at those singles events and try to find the good in what's left. Finding a job in a hurry is like that.

I didn't like champagne much, so I drank cold tall boys from 6- packs that lived in my refrigerator next to a half-eaten store-bought cake. The light bulb was burned out in my refrigerator, but you didn't need a lightbulb for cold beer and cake.

The marriage train had run me over twice already, and I was slipping farther down the best of what's left scale.

I had a last, couple hundred-dollar paycheck from the half week I wrestled the machine before I gave that factory the finger.

I paid the rent for the old growing feeble two-bedroom house. It was $550. I spent utility money on liquor, pills, and ass, and with my shrinking stormy day fund, I was down to $250. If I was careful with it, that was almost enough for two weeks of booze, smokes, and chocolate cake.

I'd gotten a late notice for the electric bill last week and one for the gas bill yesterday. But it was the first late notice for each, and you never had to pay attention til the third notice. You get the third notice, you better hope your phone is still on, so you can start calling and scheming a plan to keep your utilities on. But I still had a few weeks, and I was already skimming the For Rent classifieds, looking for more affordable digs.

Newspapers were cheap. 50 cents on the weekdays. A buck and a half for the Sunday edition. The Sunday edition was packed with hundreds of dollars of coupon savings for those that could afford to save on hundred-dollar teeth whitening programs and had enough disposable income to afford a set of collectible Elvis Presley plates.

I still buy the Sunday edition a few times a year. It's often the only ink and paper edition left in large parts of America, and that makes my heart sad. Most of the other days of the week "print" their issues on the internet now.

The Sunday edition has a big, full-color comics section. We called it the Sunday funnies in my childhood living room and we all fought over who got the funnies first. The Sunday funnies were often the only funny, in my childhood home all week.

Like everything else in an ever-changing American dreamscape, the Sunday funnies then are not the Sunday funnies now.

Americans started getting their news on the internet. The internet plugged wires into all the libraries and all the museums. You can answer any question at the snap of a finger. But the internet does not have any morals. The internet is not required to tell people what truth is and what is fiction, and somewhere along the timeline of recent human evolution we've hit a breaking point. So many Americans have believed so many fiction stories that no one has faith in the news anymore.

Newspapers were already struggling because they operate in a eat or be eaten Wall Street Shark- World. Big corporations and Wall Street investment firms started buying all the newspapers in all the American cities and towns. They did this to prove they were the sharks, and not to be eaten.

With most of the newspapers in America owned by Wall Street corporate farms all of them lost their hometown flavor, and Americans stopped caring about their hometowns and declared social media civil wars over who should be president.

Americans stopped buying newspapers, and Wall Street corporate farms have to grow more profits every year or else fear becoming the "to be eaten." They started slashing jobs on news staffs and started farming all their printing needs out of town to giant corporate printers, and that cost all the towns and cities a lot of good, union pay-scale printing jobs. Never mind the men and women out front of the newspaper building walking back and forth carrying protest signs and singing strike songs. Never mind the workers with 20-year limps, mad as all hell, their dreams of an upcoming pension slashed in those Wall Street savings. 20 more years of starting over in another factory for them, if their knees and American spirit can hold up.

Wall Street corporate farms are machines, and machines don't have emotions. They're built to produce, produce, produce, and they consume all the resources around them to maintain that production.

The Wall Street corporate farms slashed so much of the heart out of the newspapers that they became a shell of their former selves, and Americans stopped reading newspapers that weren't newspapers anymore.

The Sunday editions used to be so fat I couldn't roll them up and rubber band them when I delivered papers as a kid. Now, the Sunday edition has lost so much heart and appetite that's it's down to a third of the pages it used to be, but it still has the same amount of paid advertising. More advertising, even. The Sunday edition is printed with a fake-front page paid-advertisement now. The mother-fucking heartless Wall Street sharks sold the last sacred thing the newspaper had to sell, the front page of the Sunday edition.

The Sunday funnies have starved so much they're down to half their old size and they've sold some of that sacred space to paid ads, too.

That makes my heart sad. There's thousands of kids in living rooms in America that don't ever see the Sunday funnies anymore. And the ones that do only get a third of the funny we used to get. And what if that is all the funny they have in their home all week, like it was in my childhood home?

Some days, the cold tall boys drink like an old Merle Haggard song. Cold truth, steel guitar hymns that show you the sad. Hymns that remind you, you were born of the sad things. Hymns that encourage you that if you can hang on til next month, you can afford a new pair of good work boots, and a new, good pair of work boots will make you a new man for a week.

Or maybe Merle Haggard songs and cold beer, only drink like hymns to me.

45.

It was the day of the country church potluck benefit for Joe's family to help with the wear and tear on them from having a kid with cancer. A kid with cancer is pretty much the saddest shit on planet Earth.

Well, kids with cancer, and those sad ass abandoned puppy commercials asking for $19.99 a month. I can't stomach those commercials no more. I change the channel.

No matter how tough you are, kids with cancer are the saddest sad. When it's your buddy's kid, you can't change the channel. You gotta put your nice T shirt on and show up for support.

I rode with Lorenzo the 45 miles out of town to the country church. Tristan couldn't make it. He had to cover a shift at the record store. He sends his love, though, Lorenzo said.

Half of Joe's neighbors in the whole rural county of rural Ohio villages showed up. The fashion style for the benefit was heavy on khaki pants or jeans and John Deere trucker hats for young and old men. It was floral print dresses on the older ladies and designer jeans and farmer brand blouses for the younger ones.

There was a balloon animal clown that might have been a little drunk. I hoped he was a little drunk. Or else he was weird as fuck. Hard to tell with clowns. It's a different art form for sure. The maybe drunk country clown had a John Deere Trucker hat on, and he could only make giraffe and wiener dog balloon animals.

There was one country soccer mom and her teen daughter, trying to keep up painting cartoon characters on kids' faces. Why we paint pictures on kids faces at festivals, I don't know, but we do. There were 12 kids waiting in line. The face paint was more popular than wiener dog balloons.

There was a flat bed trailer in the back of the country church parking lot. It served as a stage for a couple of ragtag Ohio village bands on hand to provide entertainment that no one in Ohio seems to care about.

There were raffles, gift baskets, prizes, and there must have been two dozen tables full of casseroles, cookies, potato salad, and dinner rolls. There wasn't no store-bought fried chicken in sight.

There must have been two dozen types of casseroles on display. If you weren't careful, you'd almost think you were at a casserole bake off. If everyone wasn't trying to smile and make small talk in the hanging fog of a kid with cancer, maybe it *could* have been a casserole bake off.

Midwestern church folk are serious about potlucks, and they're serious about their fucking casseroles. I've frequented churches way more than one would imagine a nonbeliever would. It's like that in America. Our communities are so ingrained with church and Jesus, we can't fully escape it even if we try. And I have tried.

Midwestern church folks take their casseroles so serious that I've seen grandmothers swing purses as assault weapons arguing with other grandmothers over a casserole. Must be something Jesus said about casseroles in the Bible. I must have missed it. Or maybe it's not in the copy the Gideons provide for free.

Me and Lorenzo gave some cash away. I gave a little even though I didn't have a lot. It goes like that in America, too. The most generous always seem to have the least, and the ones that have the most in America? They're on the internet news headlines every day, legendary for skipping taxes and planting new and aggressive cancers all over earth.

Me and Lorenzo found Joe. He was looking uncomfortable in starched khakis that were a little too long, so the back cuffs dragged the ground behind him. It's hard to find pants when you're short and stocky.

We said hi, but he was busy telling church people how thankful he was for their prayers, their casseroles, and their dollar bills.

Me and Lorenzo went off to the back of the church kinda. We didn't fit in out here with the country folk and John Deere Jesus.

The country church, its brick house for the preacher man, and the parking lot, all of it was surrounded by corn fields.

Me and Lorenzo were sneaking hits off pocket flasks we'd smuggled in past the Christian temperance movement.

I noticed one of the bands was different. I heard something familiar from my teen years.

"What the hell?" I said to Lorenzo.

"Yep," he said. "I'll be damned."

The band was covering a Cramps song. I first found the Cramps at this old record store in Illinois. The record store didn't sell records when I was a teen. The record store sold cassette tapes. The guy that owned the record store was an old hippie with long white hair. He knew me and a couple other of the local hooligans were into punk pretty hard. In the middle of nowhere, Midwestern Illinois, we were desperate to get our ears, and hearts set on fire, by anything punk.

Then we found hip hop, and we dived into that for a while.

Me and Lorenzo went over by the flat bed stage that no one was paying attention to, and there was a band with a they/them singer, but we didn't know anything about they/them much then. Not even me and Lorenzo.

The lead singer had make-up on, which wasn't strange, unless your audience was wearing John Deere trucker hats.

"Good thing no one cares about music in the rural Midwest," I said to Lorenzo.

"Yeah, this is something," Lorenzo was smiling.

Later, after the pretty decent punk band was done almost blaspheming capitalism right in country Jesus' parking lot, me and Lorenzo and Joe caught up with them out by their van behind the country church.

Joe had snuck away from telling people thank you. You could tell he wasn't doing so hot, but we were Midwestern men, so we didn't talk about it.

Me, Lorenzo and Joe lit a blunt and passed it to the make-up wearing punk singer. Lorenzo at 6'5" could see over the band's van. He kept watch for any John Deere Christians. Best not to get caught smoking the devil's lettuce. Not by gun toting Ohio Christians.

We passed a flask. Joe looked a little better.

The punk band lead singer said his name was JD.

I said, "Seems an interesting place to try out new original punk anthems."

He smiled. Said, "Where the fuck else in rural Ohio is a punk band gonna gig."

I said, "Good point."

We drank some. Finished the blunt. It's like that in rural Midwest. Birds of a punk or drug feather, flock together. Even at country church benefits for kids with cancer.

JD said that like most Americans 9/11 had fucked him up a little. Said his band broke up over a woman. Said he'd nearly checked out a few times but another woman had saved him.

Lorenzo was telling the bass player and guitar player some stories about Bob Dylan, the Grateful Dead, and the free love '60s. Joe was happy to not be saying thank you, and happy to not think about his kid that had cancer, if even for a minute. Nobody mentioned Vietnam or factory cancer.

The sun was starting to fall past late afternoon country Ohio cornfields. Another band was on the flat bed. We couldn't see them, but we could hear them covering Joe Diffie and Vince Gill songs. Lucky the music was too loud and covered the vocals some. Hard to cover Vince Gill.

JD said he was up to visit for a week. He was down in Kentucky now. But he used to live in Ohio, and he was trying to get his old band kickstarted again. I told him I was trying to be a poet but hadn't kickstarted anything much in a while.

We drained our last flask. Lorenzo and Joe were talking about the Red Hot Chili Peppers with the band members.

JD didn't have a cell phone and I was scraping to keep mine on. He wrote down his address for me. Told me to write him sometime.

Me and Lorenzo stayed for about an hour after that, then split. We passed a bottle back and forth on the way home.

"Want to hit the Bucket?" I said.

"Nah. I'm sad. Kind of want to get drunk at home with Tristan," Lorenzo said.

"You like him," I said. Half question. Half statement.

Lorenzo didn't say nothing for about a half a mile. We were coasting into the edge of town. Back to stoplights, police sirens, and what is supposed to be civilization.

"You know," Lorenzo said, "I do. He's as smart as he his cute, and that mouth of his."

I didn't say anything.

"Well, his mouth that way, too," Lorenzo said.

And I had to tell him the stoplight had changed to a go-light, because he was a little drunk, glassy eyed, and smiling.

46.

I had to go downtown at 9am one morning for a child support hearing. I'd been to hearings of all types, including the aforementioned skirmishes with Uncle Sam's finest in blue cop suits. I'd never been to a child support hearing, yet though.

I put my best Levi's on. Wore one of my two button up shirts, tucked in, just in case this hearing had a God Judge with strict dress code commandments.

My brown work belt matched my brown work boots, and they were better footwear for a hearing than my only other pair of shoes, a pair of beat up black, fading to gray, Chuck Taylor tennis shoes. One shoe had a frayed hole in the side. The other had a broken shoestring that was permanently knotted at the half-shoe point for quick putting on and taking off. The Chuck's had been quick on and off so many times they'd been beaten to three months past their recommended use, and their tongues were limp and twisted, and flopped when you walked.

Battered to hell brown work boots were the only option.

My Levi's were my most recent new pair, and I never wore my newest pair to work. I saved them for blind dates or court. Other higher moral, low working-class factory men save their best jeans for church or weddings.

I'd read in *Esquire* once that a man's belt should match his shoes. I used to read *Esquire,* when I was homeless and loitered around the library. I was glad my belt matched my boots. The library would be proud.

Might would give me a library card now.

The child support hearing was in a tall eight story brick government building. It was across the street from the big courthouse, where me and the woman suing me for child support had been married in a stairwell.

On the other side of the big fancy civil war era architecture style courthouse, was the city courthouse for misdemeanors. Two blocks up from that was the county jail. Behind it, a four-story police headquarters.

At 26 years of age, and two years of being a Toledo resident, I'd managed to visit all those government buildings. They didn't give me any frequent flyer lowlife discounts, and my luck was progressively worse the more I visited.

The mother of my daughters strolled up the sidewalk laughing, a big, oversized leather purse on her shoulder, and carrying a chain store cup of coffee worth an hour of draft beers at the Bucket. She had on a black pant dress suit with jacket and purple blouse. She wore black wedge heels. Her make-up was nice. She had big lips, and she wore lip puffer lip gloss. Her hair was fresh cut, long and layered, and bounced behind her as she came walking down the downtown block owned by the government. Pop anthem soundtracks might have played behind her if we weren't in Toledo.

My baby mama looked alright with her $300 south Toledo makeover. She might had lost 10 pounds. Might have been the black suit.

Baby mama strolled up the downtown block with an entourage. She had a hot blonde and tan 30-year-old woman with her. I knew she was a lawyer, and I think they're still fair game for stereotyping. She was tall, 5'10ish. On the right side of thick. In the neighborhood of 170 pounds. Guessing women's weights ain't no safe place for a man writer to venture. No matter how tough I think I am.

She had a hot lawyer strolling with her. And both her parents were with her.

The lawyer lady walked up and handed me her business card right there outside the government bricks.

137

She said, "Do not contact my client. We intend to file an order of protection."

I exhaled cigarette smoke in her face. I hadn't planned to do that when I'd inhaled, but the opportunity presented itself, and I blew smoke in her face.

She didn't flinch. She was tougher than I thought.

She stood her ground and said, "Mr. No Good Lowlife, you're a violent, mentally ill, piece of shit alcoholic, and an overall shit stain on society. I intend to soak you dry and help my client rid herself of your stench."

She said something like that.

I laughed. Said, "Shit, Lady, you got all that straight without interviewing me. You must cost a whole week's worth of Bucket beers per lawyer hour."

She ushered her client inside the government door. Baby mama's ass was still too big, but with the wedge heels it wobbled twice per step, and I felt my heart almost smile at the memory of it. If my heart didn't have cotton mouth it might have smiled watching that ass wobble.

The in laws that didn't want to be my in laws anymore, skirted wide and inside to safety.

I finished my smoke. Stubbed it out in a government ash tray. Looked down at the sexy lawyer's business card.

I tell you this without judgement. It said, all men are scum.

We all made it through the plastic government metal detector security ritual. I had to be scanned by hand wand. Hand scanner under my arms, around my crotch, and it was the steel in my steel toe boots trying to smuggle themselves in. They gave me a hall pass on the offensive boots.

The hearing was in a big government office. It was painted government white. There was a big government desk in the front. A government table with four government chairs, one set for each team in the war room.

There was a big state seal on the front wall behind the big government desk. The government seal said this state's motto was "In God We Trust." I didn't have a fucking friend in sight.

I was at one government table by myself. I was empty handed. A half pack of Kool's in my front pocket, my only back up.

The hearing was presided over by a family services case worker. She had a county cop for an assistant. With the four county cops in the metal detector lobby squad and one per hearing, they had a whole fucking armed infantry. Government buildings have been like that since Oklahoma City was terrorized, and they've been re-armed with military weapons since the American dream was murdered on 9/11.

Free citizens protected by military enforcement is a weird democracy to live in. No one cared for that opinion though. Not at the child support hearing.

The family services social worker was late 50s and looked like she had been overworked with family services cases since her first day out of college. She looked like she was four years behind on vacation days and six years behind in naps.

She asked the lawyer if she was representing my baby mama and if she had all the required papers to smash my ass.

The sexy lawyer that wasn't much into dudes said they surely did.

The social worker asked me why I didn't have a lawyer.

I said, "I don't have money for a lawyer."

She said, "You have a right to one."

I said, "All the government buildings tell me I have a right to a lawyer, but I have almost never had any money for one."

She said, "Sucks to be you Mr. Lowlife."

She said, "How's come you didn't bring any papers like we told you to."

I said, "I ain't got papers to bring. I sort of got let go at the factory. I ain't got a job. No money. No paycheck coming next week."

I said, "I think she took our tax papers. And I'm fucked every which way to next factory job at the moment."

Social worker said, "Sucks to be you Mr. Lowlife."

I said, "It surely does. Plus, she won't let me see my daughters. Can you put that on the record?"

Social worker said, "This is child support. We tell you how much it costs to be a dad in America. We don't have any concerns with visitation."

I said, "I have some fucking concerns."

The county cop said, "Hey watch your mouth."

Nobody said anything.

The social worker said, "Mr. Lowlife, the mother of your daughters is asking for $150 a week in child support. That doesn't seem unreasonable for two daughters. Especially since she says she doesn't have a job."

The lawyer proved she was there to earn her high dollar salary. She said, "And furthermore social worker lady, my client is unable to work at this time. She's in therapy for emotional duress inflicted by this lowlife at the other table. He left her high and dry with no money. He was abusive. Look at him. He's a goddamn heathen piece of shit."

It seemed like that's what she said.

I said, "Hey. That ain't fair. I object."

The social worker lady said, "This ain't court stupid. You can't object."

I said, "Well I do object. I ain't never hit that bitch one fucking time. I yell a lot, sure, but she was always throwing shit and making our daughters cry."

The county cop yelled, and said, "I told you once to watch your mouth."

I said, "Nobody asked you motherfucker."

I didn't intend to say that to the county cop. The opportunity presented itself, and I did say it.

He pushed a button on his walkie-talkie and raced over and tackled me.

It was easy to tackle me because I was still sitting in my government chair.

The county cop came across the table, arms wrapped around me in perfect NFL football tackle, and we went flying against the wall. The government chair broke. They aren't built to support anything of substance. Certainly not dying American dreams.

By the time the county cop had his handcuffs out, six county cops were entering swat team style, and four of them held me down with their knees on my back while four of them checked and rechecked to make sure the handcuffs were sufficiently cutting off the blood supply to my hands. Four and four? Fuck. I lost track of my "I'm fucked math."

They put me in a government closet sized room with two government chairs.

I sat there for a half a 12-hour factory shift with my hands cuffed so tight I hadn't felt them since first break. Those hours were some of the longest hours I've ever lived. Longer than factory hours. Heavier than hangover hours. Harder on your heart than broke-with-no-smokes, three days before payday hours.

I had to piss for the last six Mondays of the fucking ordeal. This is, I think, a form of legal torture frequently used by military county cops. I'd read in the half dead Sunday paper recently these cops just graduated from a six-week military camp, inner city counterterrorism boot camp funded by a Homeland Security grant of $360,000.

Thank god for Homeland Security grants. Otherwise, the brick government building would have surely withered under my F-bombs.

By the time the highly trained swat team came to take my handcuffs off and tell me that they had checked with every government office in every government building within six blocks, and every fucking office knew me, surprise, surprise, you fucking lowlife, you are not wanted by any of them.

While we believe you're a scum bag and clearly a waste of good oxygen, you didn't commit any crimes today.

They let me go. I had to piss so bad that my dick had gone numb from enduring a hour's long piss hard on. My bladder had stopped aching an hour ago. I was certain I'd leaked piss in my boxers three or four times, when dead hand lightning bolts of pain would shoot through my handcuffed hands.

The county cops said the government building was closing so I couldn't use their bathroom.

They said, "Oh yeah. Here's this, too. It's a restraining order. No contact with your baby mama you scum bag lowlife. She's been through enough with you already."

It felt like they said that.

I race walked behind an alley dumpster between an abandoned downtown Toledo skyscraper and a dying downtown restaurant. My hands were so numb it took me three minutes to safely get the zipper on my good Levi's down and another two to get my dick out of the fly of my boxers. I was certain I squirted piss twice in the process.

I pissed against a ghost town skyscraper for about six minutes. Halfway through a homeless man shuffled by. He stopped. He looked like he hadn't made friends with any soap for three months.

He stopped and looked at me. My dick kept draining. I looked back at the homeless man.

He said "Jesus man. What did they do to you in there? You look like shit."

I said, "You wouldn't believe it if I told you."

He laughed. His laugh sounded like he'd gargled a pack of dollar cigars for decades. My dick was heaving. My bladder spasmed with a relief that was almost as nice as an orgasm. Nothing is as nice as an orgasm is, though. No matter what they tell you.

The homeless man spit a golf-ball sized loogie. Wiped his mouth with the back of a dirty sweater sleeve. The sweater hadn't made friends with soap in so long you couldn't tell what original color it meant to be.

The homeless guy said. "Trust me. I'd believe ya. I've seen the shit those motherfuckers do to people."

He laughed some more cigarette laugh.

I tucked my dick in, zipped the Levi's. Hands stinging back to electric blood flow. It only took a minute and a half to work the zipper.

I hadn't smoked a cigarette in about eight long goddamned hours. I fumbled a Kool out of my smashed half front pocket back-up pack.

My Bic came through even with numb hands.

The homeless guy asked for a smoke.

I gave him one.

"You got any money?" He asked.

"A little."

"Nice," he said.

I gave him three singles and a second cigarette.

My boxers were still dry in my Levi's. My bladder held the line one more time.

My heart was so tired I was worried it would take an illegal nap. Tired hours are harder on a heart.

The homeless guy said his name was Shane. Said he had been waiting on his disability check to come since he tried to commit suicide in 1992.

I said, "Damn Shane. That's a long fucking time. You sure it's coming."

He said yeah. But he couldn't remember his address anymore. Said he hadn't been home since he couldn't remember when.

"What day is it?" he asked.

"Jesus," He asked. "What the fuck they do to you? You look tired."

I drove home to an empty old two-bedroom house. There was a third and final electric bill notice taped to the front door. It had orange letters.

Two weeks later, the lights were off and I got a letter in the mail that said I had to pay my baby mama $150 a week in child support. It was back-dated to the day after my second baby was born. Six fucking months. Fuck man. I was almost $4k in the hole, and I had $11 left to my name.

The lights were out. My last beers were getting warm in a dying refrigerator.

Good thing I was starting a new job next week. The last ray of hope in a tired and burned-out heart.

47.

One of the few saving graces I've had the dumb luck of having is sometimes, when my back is really against a desperate wall I can lace up the work boots, put my head down, and grind the motherfucking machines.

Sometimes I can do that, and sometimes that single minded focus of not drowning in desperation, the single focus of not slipping another rung down the economy ladder can be enough to keep me from straying too close to the edge of full-on madness. No matter if I was swimming in addiction, insanity, poverty, homelessness, whatever the fuck you want to call the river monsters that grabbed at my boots while I was wading through the stream of life.

Sometimes I could put my head down, and through sheer force of willpower, rigid discipline, born of the knowledge there ain't any safety nets below me on the economy ladder scale.

After a few weeks of reading classified help wanted ads, and putting applications in, I landed a job in another factory. I was interviewed and hired by a temporary staffing company. Temporary staffing companies are a new loophole industry. An industry created by capitalism to help Wall Street company owners save money by not having to pay health benefits, and social security taxes.

I hated working temp jobs. Some of their jobs really were temporary positions. Most of their jobs were full-time forever jobs, you just made a lot less, and didn't get benefits. Most temporary jobs like you to remember you're a temporary employee. On shaky footing from your first minutes on your first day. They like you to remember you better work hard to impress so you can be a temporary worker again tomorrow, and next week and next month. Temporary employees are easy to fire. A phone call to the staffing agency office, and someone from there will call and say you're no longer needed at your temporary job, but don't talk back to us. Accept your fate as an easy to replace temporary human, and don't make waves. We'll try to find you another temporary job next week.

After a few weeks of watching my emergency dollars bleed away and my utilities get shut off, I couldn't be picky. I was running out of ways to buy tall boys and Kool's. I took a temporary job paying $10 an hour with overtime promised every week.

The new temporary job was in a factory that put crackers in boxes. All the different kinds of crackers you could think of this factory put them in boxes.

The crackers were already made and packaged. I ran machines that folded cardboard into shiny, bright colored cracker boxes. The machines folded a box every two seconds and spit it out on a conveyer. The shiny boxes would pass by minimum wage workers whose only job was to put one package of crackers in each box, so by the end of the conveyer each shiny box would have the right amount of crackers in it.

Another machine at the end folded the box flaps down and glued them shut. Two more workers stood at the end and worked as fast as they could, stacking cracker boxes on pallets. The cracker stackers made a quarter more than minimum wage, and they could never keep up, no matter how fast they worked.

The cracker box factory hired everyone through a low-end temporary agency. All temporary agencies are low end when you're the one looking for work and not the Wall Street company owner. But this temporary job agency was in a block building in the North End of Toledo. It didn't have neon lights in the window to attract workers. It didn't have clean floors, fake plants in the lobby, or any jobs available that paid enough to break a sweat on the poverty line. This North End temporary agency only hired for jobs no one else wanted, and they only hired workers that weren't wanted anywhere else.

I'd filled out an application there, at the low-end temporary agency, and the lady sitting behind the window looked it over in less than 30 seconds. The lady had pale white skin and was shaped like a beach ball. Every way you looked at her she was round and as wide as she was tall.

She looked at my application for 30 seconds and said, "Says here you have more than two years of machine operator experience."

"That's correct," I said. Of course it was correct. I'd just written that on there.

She said, "Ok. Can you start next Monday?"

I told her I could. Easy interview.

On Monday, an HR lady met me, another guy, and two women at the front door of the cracker box factory. The HR lady said we had to wear hair nets and beard nets, because this was a food process plant.

They took me to a machine and another machine operator stopped by and said, "Push the green button to make it go, red button to stop it. Easy job."

That was all the training I received and when the bell rang the team leader in charge of the whole cracker line I was on came over and I pushed the green button, and the machine growled to life, started folding flaps and spitting out cracker boxes.

When the machine ran right, it was an easy job. All I had to do was keep fresh cardboard loaded in it and watch the machine to make sure it didn't accidentally eat itself.

The cracker packers stood in one spot, hands a blur, picking and putting cracker packages in every box. The machine operator at the other end was watching over the glue and box sealer machine. The two cracker stackers at the end were running in circles, stacking cracker boxes almost as fast as we could run them down the line.

My machine jammed up every 40 minutes. It had two glue sprayers on each side of the stack of cardboard. After the machine folded the cardboard into a box, the glue sprayers shot glue onto the sides and a conveyer took the box through a metal chute that squeezed the flaps shut over the fresh glue.

The glue kept leaking and building up, and after 40 minutes the glue build up jammed up the cardboard. When the cardboard jammed, the machine kept trying to turn cardboard into more cracker boxes every two seconds. If you didn't hit the red stop button quick, the machine would start spitting deformed boxes all over and they would spill all around the machine like a cracker box snowstorm.

The cracker box factory was a food processing plant, so we had to wear hair nets and beard nets. They weren't allowed to open any windows or have any fans to cool the plant down. They weren't supposed to have any moving air because moving air blew dust around, and dust blowing around isn't ideal for food processing.

We didn't process food, though. We just put cracker packages in cracker boxes. Didn't matter. No moving air allowed.

There were 15 cracker box packing lines, and with all those machines, and all those people, and no moving air, and the brick, cracker-box-factory became an oven every afternoon. We'd be sweating through our hair nets and beard nets, crackers and cracker boxes flying all over the place.

The cracker packers, and cracker stackers worked 10-hour shifts, but the machine operators went in a half hour early to make the machine's morning coffee and stayed a half hour late to change its diaper and give it a bath before bedtime.

The cracker packers and the cracker stackers worked Monday through Thursday getting their 40 banker's hours in a hurry every week. The machine operators worked six hours on Fridays, so they could groom their machines, give them massages, and pat them on their asses before the machines and their operators took the weekend off.

My first week in the factory I moved out of the old, tiny two-bedroom house. I didn't have any money and I could have crashed at a few places, but I didn't. I moved out of the tiny house and into my car.

It was summer, so it wasn't bad. Drove out to a truck stop on the edge of town, napped in the back seat, went back to work in the morning.

At the end of the week I didn't have a paycheck since you always got paid a week late for the work you did. I was broker than fucking broke. I was I-got-two-cigarettes to my-name-broke. Got less-than-a quarter tank-of-gas, and that's it, broke.

I came across a whole bottle of pills. How I came across them will be my own karma to answer to someday, but I got $150 for the pills. We all have our own brand of preferred medicine.

I stopped by my ex-two-bedroom house that was divorcing me. I checked the mailbox. There was mail. One of the envelopes had a reminder of my first divorce hearing. We were supposed to meet with a court mediator to see if we could negotiate our way to an easy divorce. It was next week.

My ex-house was empty, save for the ghosts that follow us all. So I snuck in the back door and took a quick bath in the claw foot tub. Someone had gotten the lights switched back on. That was nice.

I snuck back out fresh bathed and went down to the Bucket. It was Saturday happy hour, and I was off tomorrow. I had only drunk enough to sleep in a car at night, and not enough to get drunk in two weeks.

Angie wasn't there. It was the weekend. She was hanging out with her husband who wasn't her boyfriend. I drank draft beers fast for an hour. It was Saturday night, I'd made it through a whole week in the cracker box oven, and I had more than enough money to get good and fucked up. There ain't too many things better in life than giving yourself permission to get good and fucked up with just enough money to do so.

I'd saved a handful of pills hoping I'd run into my friend, the woman that lived in the rusty trailer and liked pills. She came in around 8:30. She was with some 40-year-old banker, wannabe-biker guy. Shit.

She didn't even look at me when she walked past me. I started drinking $2 shots.

I drank til midnight, and I was fucked up. I needed to fuck. My friend that liked pills had left with the banker-biker a few hours ago. I needed a different friend, so I went looking for one. I used two of my pills and a little of my cash, and me and my new friend got along just fine in the backseat of my car.

48.

My second week at the Cracker Box Factory was just like my first. Go in early and give my machine positive affirmations before the day started.

Feed fresh cardboard into it every 10 minutes all day.
Sweat through my beard net.
Watch an army of minimum wage, minimum hope-cracker packers, march cracker pack marches, 10 hours a day.
Scrape glue buildups off glue sprayers and shovel my way out of cracker box snowstorms.
Chain smoke cigarettes on 10-minute breaks.
Give the machine a sponge bath and a hug at the end of every day.

Over half of the cracker packers were Hispanic, and over half of them didn't speak English. There were a couple Hispanic machine operators, and one of the two big bosses was Hispanic. He didn't speak much English either.

I didn't say much to anyone my first week, even though I'd collected a few dozen Spanish words in my vocabulary over the years. I've learned to take a low profile until I get the lay of the land.

Every factory that I've ever called home has had its own wavelength. Its own energy and local flavor, and none of them like the new guy. The new guy sticks out, and no factory has ever cared for anyone that stands out.

Factories are like school yards in that way. Or a little like jail. They're all tough places to survive, and they all bear their own brand of institutionalization. The factory is similar to jail in that it's likely the new guy is going to have to stand up for himself at least once, and pretty quick to fit in. If you don't, one of two things is going to happen: you're gonna get taken advantage of, or you ain't gonna make it. It's been like that in my schoolyard tour, and in my trauma fueled broken tour of a few jails, and a whole lot of motherfucking factories. It gets so a man living a hard life feels like he's always in a new spot so much, that he's always got to stand up to someone to prove he's not to be taken advantage of.

I didn't say much that first week, but by the second, I was getting to know my cracker assembly line well enough that I could joke with Tina, the team leader, while we chain smoked at break time. Tina was mid 30s, tall and as skinny as the cigarettes she chain-smoked. She had bleached blonde hair and a face that told tough times stories. Tina had three kids and a crackhead old man that went off the rails once every three months.

Tina wasn't married to her old man, but they'd been together since high school, and now two of their kids were in high school and one in junior high. Them kids never stood a chance at getting ahead in life, cuz their dad fell off the crack wagon once every three months.

Tina lived on menthol cigarettes and caffeine. Me and her and Jayvon, whose last name was Jones, so we all called him Jonesy, all lived the same factory diet. Cigarettes and coffee on first break. Cigarettes and an energy drink for lunch. Cigarettes and a Mountain Dew on our afternoon break.

Jonesy was the machine operator that ran the glue machine at the end. The machine that sealed the cracker boxes shut. Jonesy was a big black guy, probably 6 foot 300 pounds, and was in his early 20s. He had one toddler son with a baby momma that he wasn't married to either. Maybe if I hadn't of married my baby mama we'd still be together, swimming through back street Toledo desperation. Maybe not getting married was the key to long term success, down here underneath the poverty line.

Jonesy loved music. He had headphones around his neck all the time. He was gonna be a rapper, but he'd been arrested three times for selling weed already and kept dropping dirty on probation, so he was stuck here in cracker purgatory with the rest of us unfortunates.

Factories aren't just waiting rooms for those that don't know what they aspire to be in adulthood. They're also bus stops for those that can't afford the ever-rising bus fare. Those that can't ever get on the bus that goes to the suburbs. Every time Jonesy thought he was about to get his little family onto the bus that leads to being someone, Uncle Sam's cops hauled him back to jail for selling marijuana.

Me and Tina and Jonesy all had to be at work 30 minutes before all the other workers on our cracker box line, so we spent extra minutes together, and we already spent more minutes with cracker boxes than we spent with those we were working to take care of.

That second week, I smoked, drank caffeine, and filled my low paying role in a billion-dollar cracker enterprise. I'd wander around in the evening. Stop at the library and sneak past library clerks that wouldn't issue me a passport to travel home with any books. I didn't have an address again. I could only get a work visa in our nation's hallowed libraries. I could visit for the day, but I had to leave for home empty handed. Or was supposed to. That's the thing about supposed to's. They matter less when you're poor, even though the consequences of doing not supposed-tos cost us more.

I'd wind up out at the truck stop on the edge of town at night. They had showers at the truck stop. It cost $6 to take a shower, and $6 is a day's cigarettes, or a nighttime bottle of help-you-sleep, poor man's whiskey, and that was a necessity for being able to fall asleep in the back seat of your car after an 11-hour shift of being kicked in the teeth by cracker boxes.

I paid the $6 for the shower one night anyway. It was almost worth it. I stood for 30 minutes, smoking three cigarettes, and letting industrial-strength-hot, truck stop water almost wash away a week's worth of living in my car.

Hot showers are like physical therapy for factory workers. They're like spiritual therapy for homeless motherfuckers like me. Being able to scrub your armpits, balls, and asshole clean enough to eat off of is almost heaven. Cleanliness is next to godliness, they say, and most cliches have just enough gospel to keep us repeating them even when we no longer go to church.

A 30-minute hot shower won't wash your heart though. Or your brain. Hot showers can burn your asshole clean, but it can't wash away the shit that's been put in your head.

Baptisms may get you to Heaven, but they won't change the chemistry of your brain. I don't know why more people don't understand that.

I only showered that once the second week. Went back to wiping my underarms, and balls in the truck stop bathroom sinks. That's not uncommon in truck stops. Even $1000 a week and home-every-weekend truckers don't like to pay $6 for a shower. Can't wash your asshole in a truck stop sink though. Not without standing out too much. Best to not stick out here either.

I had to stand up for myself in the middle of the second week. I was smoking on the patio at lunch. The patio was a concrete pad surrounded by an 8-foot chain-link fence that was topped with barbed wire. It had a half dozen industrial strength wooden picnic tables with various disabilities, and one long bench along one side that had a half bus stop bus station roof over it. The patio was located off the front of the cracker box factory, so that a hundred factory workers would be loitering around, eating, smoking, and talking on cell phones that were still more phones than anything else.

There was a four-lane busy road in front of the cracker box factory, so that every day we'd be out there looking like restless cracker inmates while Toledo traffic and Toledo life streamed past, mostly ignoring us.

Tina was on her half brick cell phone checking to make sure her old man hadn't fallen off the crack wagon. Jonesy was nearby but talking about weed with another worker.

I was wearing a Marilyn Manson T shirt I'd got at the Goodwill for 50 cents. One of the cracker packers from another cracker line said something about Marilyn Manson being a tranny, and the three other packers nearby laughed.

I didn't say anything. Just smoked my square. Kinda wished my cell phone service hadn't been cut off. Might would have been nice to have called Lorenzo at lunch. Or Joe. Or my friend that liked pills, to see if she needed any pills, or any friendship.

The packer from the other line said something else, louder, and six people laughed.

The packer said, "Hey. You into that weird, freako tranny stuff?"

He was a white guy with kitchen tattoos and prison tattoos.

"Fuck you, man. Just a shirt," I said.

"I heard Marilyn Manson got a rib taken out so he could suck his own dick," The packer said. Eight people laughed.

"What kind of fag sucks his own dick?" the packer asked. 10 people laughed.

"You like to suck dicks?" the packer asked.

"Why? You lonely?" I said.

It got quiet a second.

"Fuck you. I ain't a faggot. I get bitches all the time," he said. 12 people chuckled and looked at me.

Tina walked over. She was lighting another cigarette, holding an energy drink can under her armpit.

"What the fuck is going on?" she said.

"Romeo here was telling us how big his dick is, but none of us believe him," I said.

Tina busted out laughing and coughing cigarette smoke.

12 people laughed with her.

"Shit, motherfucker. I'll show you how big," the packer said.

But no one was laughing with him anymore.

We walked back into the cracker factory when the first bell rang. A one-minute warning that the cracker box machine was about to wake up from his 30-minute noon nap, and start spitting cracker boxes, and the factory time clock was about to start counting more factory hours on my heart's odometer, an odometer already reading high mileage. Factory miles are harder than highway miles. My heart was fading to "good runner" at best. It got me by, but it wasn't pretty to drive.

49.

I went to the cracker factory and let the machine make crumbs of my heart. I laced boots up, put my head down, and showed up.

I'd missed the mediation appointment for divorce court, and someone was living in my ex-house. Story of my life. All my exes move on quick. My ex-house having new tenants meant that I couldn't get my mail. I didn't know what was going on down there at divorce court anymore. I'm sure I had another appointment coming, but hell if I knew when.

I risked a quarter in a truck stop pay phone, my third week of learning to swim in cracker dust and learning to live in the backseat of a car again.

I called my wife's parents' house. My wife's mom answered.

I said, "Is my wife there?"

She didn't say anything.

22 seconds later my wife said "What?"

"Are you still my wife?"

"Fuck you," she said.

"But you didn't much anymore," I said. And she hung up on me.

I still didn't know if she was still my wife. Was I married? Or not. Purgatory is a rough motherfucking neighborhood to live in. Not knowing who you are or where you are on the American caste system is a tough spot for anyone, no matter which truck stop is nearest. I didn't know if I was fading husband or homeless derelict. There's a difference in self respect.

My third week of not collecting any mail at the truck stop, after I made my noble attempt to find out my status in life, I took my weekly, fuck-it, it's only $6, truck stop shower.

I took my backpack in with sweatpants, shower gel, shampoo, and deodorant from the nearest sad-faced dollar store. You know, the ones that live on every corner now. You know, the dollar stores that sport 50 cent promises. The dollar stores that sell sardines in mustard, five tin-cans for a dollar. I was living on them sardines in mustard. They were made in China. Sardines taste like the rubber bicycle inner tubes of seafood. Sardines taste so much like fish, that you can still taste the fish until three teeth brushings have passed. They can't be back-to-back teeth brushings either. That don't work. You can't rush the sardines away.

The best way to live on sardines is to have crackers and strong liquor. Thunderbird red wine is a good choice. A big bottle is $4 or some shit. Thunderbird ain't the kind of wine anyone with hope or free checking accounts would drink.

The cracker factory gave away free orphaned cracker packs that had fallen on hard factory floor, and told they had no value to society until a hungry enough cracker factory employee rescued them and gave them a purpose.

I snagged a few tubes of the good circle crackers. A whole tube, and two twenty cent cans of sardines in mustard from the we're on every nearest corner but no one wants to shop here dollar store, you know the one. A circle tube of the good crackers and two cans of sardines, a $4 big bottle of poor man's prayers in the backseat of a two door, smashed up, rusted down '91 Cavalier under two truck stop parking lot lights with light bulbs more tired than a street whore the morning after factory payday, and that's how you save money for a future apartment on a temporary-job, shoe-string factory budget.

I took my $6 weekly shower that third week after my maybe still, maybe not wife, hung up on me and wasted my quarter.

I smoked cigarettes under water set to warm but not hot. Washed as much of who I had turned out to be away, as I could.

I was standing at the truck stop bathroom sink at midnight brushing my teeth. My hair was wet. I had sweatpants on. I hadn't put my t shirt on yet. I was free balling under the sweatpants. It's hot as fuck in the cracker factory for 11 hours a day. My balls were happy to hang loose all night.

A 38-year-old truck driver came in the weeknight, midnight quiet truck stop bathroom. I finger combed my hair. It was four weeks past the warranty on its last haircut, and my beard was shaggy.

The trucker was done draining his lizard and he showed up at the sink next to mine. I knew that wasn't right. There were seven sinks. Men aren't supposed to do this in bathrooms. I tried not to look. Shut the sink off. Find the paper towels.

"I'll give you $50 if you let me suck your dick," he said.

I looked over and he had his dick out of his fly and he was jacking off. He had a big ugly fat dick that was crooked by the head a little to the left.

I report all of this without judgement. I've made my own midnight offers.

"No thanks, man," I said. I tried not to pay attention to him jacking off.

"I'm not a fag," the trucker said.

"Ok," I said. I put my t shirt on fast. Started putting stuff in my backpack.
The trucker grunted.

"You don't like getting your dick sucked?" The trucker asked. "I'm good at it."

"I believe you." I said, stuffing my naked feet into tired work boots.

"Fuck you, man. I'm not a fucking fag." He said.

"Ok," I said.

"I got a wife," he said. "Two kids," he said.

"That's nice," I said, walking towards the bathroom door.

The trucker was jacking off fast now.

"I'll swallow" he said.

I locked the cavalier doors three times that night.

Couldn't sleep. Hadn't fucked in eight days or something. Hadn't fucked in a bed in a month.

My dick wouldn't shut the fuck up. I jacked off slow, my hand in my sweatpants. I thought about my might be wife. The way she always wore this shiny lip gloss that made her big lips look fat and shiny. I thought about how her mouth was always wet. Jesus. So fucking wet.

Slow strokes on raging hard still twenty something cock

I thought about my might be wife. The way she refused to use her hands. The way she knew to get on her knees. To make eye contact. The way she always swallowed.

She told me once that it made her feel pretty when she sucked dicks. She said she knew men liked it. She said she practiced it on her Christian counselor at Christian summer camp, three summers in a row. Twice a day, every day, for six weeks, she'd been almost proud to tell me.

It started when she was 11.

"He wouldn't fuck me," she said. When she told me her dirty stories, she liked to say dirty words. "he said I should save that for someone special. I thought it meant he loved me."

He was 19 that first summer, and I won't give you anymore of the sick fucking details. Not my story to sell you or tell you.

I'll tell you this though, that last summer that clean cut, Bible quoting Christian camp counselor that was so anal retentive that he ironed his Levi's and taught my future ex-wife how to iron blue jeans, that sick motherfucker was 22. She was 14. He turned mean that last summer she told me. He grew up. Wasn't ashamed of sex anymore.

"Of course. I found out later he had a fiancée back home in rural Indiana." She said. "I was just a stupid 14-year-old. He was cheating on me."

He talked her into doing things that 14-year-old girls shouldn't probably know about, although almost all my lovers, short and long term, paid for with cash or shaky credit, have done those things by 14.

I knew about them at 14, too. And did them before I knew their cost.

There's no reason to boast of it. Scars caused, and scars earned, are lessons, not trophies.

I thought about how my maybe ex wife used to tell me dirty stories. She liked to tell me stories that made me mad. She liked it that I got mad thinking about some other man shoving his dick her mouth. She told me once, back before our first daughter showed up, and we didn't know each other enough to hate each other yet. Back when we still talked. When we were still trying to impress each other by proving how rough we could fuck. She told me it made her feel clean when I got mad and hurt her when we fucked.

She used to tell me stories about being bored, and lonely. Stuck in school. Stuck living at home and working part time in a nursing home.

Stuck helping old ladies that had families too busy to care for them play bingo before having their afternoon pudding cup. The old ladies asked her every day if she had a boyfriend. When was she going to have babies?

She took me there once, to the nursing home. We'd been together 90 days. She smiled at those old ladies and told them she was gonna be a mom. She smiled and said, "Look how handsome my boyfriend is. He works so hard." She said, "yes he does take good care of me."

She told me she would go to random bars. Flirt and get men to buy her drinks. She would get drunk. Offer to suck strange men's dicks in their car in dive bar parking lots.

"One guy liked to cum on my face and make me drive home without washing it off."

I hated her. I hated her. My heart hurts but there's too many secrets.

I jacked off thinking about that story she told me. Thinking about how she liked to get naked and iron my work jeans. How she liked to role-play being 14 again. "Be a little mean, Daddy," she'd say. Then she'd tell me dirty stories about her past until I couldn't help it anymore, and I was mean to both of us.

I jacked off thinking about paying her to let me fuck her face. Hate. Hate. Hate.

I'm middle aged now. 15 years served on a lifetime ban from strong medicinal wine. 15 years of therapy, and a lifetime of reading books to prove how smart I can be, and I'm just now learning the cost of living these secrets. I'm learning the cost of stolen and traded pleasure.

Two thousand sleepless nights haven't brought back the parts of me I gave away. No matter how many times I baptize myself in midnight ghost town showers, I can't wash away the secrets forced into me. I can't wash away another man's sins.

50.

The cracker packing factory was a boring, desperate place. With so many of the workers speaking a different language, there was about half the normal factory chatter here. The highest paid workers made $14 an hour top pay, and only a handful of team leaders had been around long enough to top out. No one had any money here.

The machine that made cracker boxes was needy as fuck. You couldn't take your eye off it too long, or else it would start spitting cracker boxes out sideways and deformed. You'd have it running good, turn around to look at the young girl on the next line over. The young girl that wore yoga pants every day. The girl that all the guys said looked better from the back.

You'd be wondering what color that girl's thong was today, and the cracker box machine would bite your leg, and puke an avalanche of twisted boxes.

You'd get your snowstorm of broken-flap, cracker boxes cleaned up, and you'd watch the machine, just waiting for it to act up again, and it would run just fine for an hour, until you turned your back.

The cracker packing factory hours piled just as heavy as all the other factories, so the odometer on my heart racked 1.5 hours for every hour I was there.

I made it through another week, and I went to see Lorenzo at his wizard bookstore. He was there by himself. He broke out a new bottle of Jack, cracked it open, hit it, and passed it to me. I hit it like it was the medicine it was. The medicine I needed.

"Don't tell Tristan we drank out of the bottle," Lorenzo said. "He's been trying to break me of it."

"He ain't heard about the old dogs, new tricks thing, huh?" I asked.

I asked how Joe was, and I wished I hadn't. Joe's daughter didn't take to the aggressive treatment. It wasn't gonna go well, Lorenzo told me.

We drank more. Talked a little about some books. A little about love. A little about life.

"How's your divorce going?" Lorenzo asked.

"Who knows?" I told him.

Everything else we talked about after talking about Joe, and Joe's kid, felt like small talk. Neither me, nor Lorenzo, much cared for small talk.

I left and went over to the Bucket. My heart felt like it had been left out in a week's worth of cold rainstorms.

My friend that liked pills was at the Bucket. Angie wasn't. It was the weekend.

My friend that liked pills had a black eye that had turned yellow. She looked like she had aged six years since last month.

I bought her a drink. She told me she needed some pills.

I told her I didn't have any.

"Well, you're about as worthless as shit, ain't ya," she said and she slammed the drink I bought her and got up and left.

"Fuck you, too, lady," I said, and bought myself another shot and mason jar beer.

51.

I finally found an apartment my fourth week tending cracker box machines. It was in a giant 120-year-old house in the north end. The house had been turned into four apartments, and mine was in the back on the ground floor facing an alley.

The back door was the only way in and it had been kicked in so many times that it flinched when we approached it. The window of the door had a black metal grate over it. Behind the grate was the front of a Cheerio's box someone had taped over the window where the glass was supposed to be.

My new digs had a beat up and depressed kitchen, big living room with shag carpet that had been set on fire in two spots, and a large bedroom. All the rooms had radiator heaters with an inch of layered paint flaking off. The ceilings were 12 foot high.

All the windows had black metal grates over them.

The bathroom was brand new, though.

"Just had my handyman re-do it," the two-bit landlord told me. He worked at one of the big east side refineries. They made big union money there.

The bathroom was put together with discount rack pieces that were so new they still had the discount rack price tags on them.

Rent was $325 a month.

"You handy?" The landlord asked.

"Huh?"

"I work a lot. The window on the door needs fixing, kitchen needs work, and the carpet needs to be replaced in the living room eventually," he said.

Three out of eight cabinets were missing doors in the kitchen, and three more had broken hinges and hung so crooked that one of them was bound to run for Congress.

The gas stove was missing two burners and two knobs and its digital clock didn't know what time it was, so it gave up telling the time and stared back with a blank look. The refrigerator sounded like it had emphysema when it kicked on.

"Looks like someone had a bonfire on the carpet," I said.

"Yeah. Last tenant's old lady set his clothes on fire in a big pile." He shrugged.

"That explains the new paint on the ceiling."

"Yeah, that was a mess. Made $1750 on the insurance claim though. Paid out the middle of three professional quotes and I hired a crackhead dry wall guy for $5 an hour." The landlord laughed.

"Shit. This place only cost me four grand. America, the land of opportunity." The landlord laughed.

I negotiated a free deposit and $250 first month's rent for replacing the carpet and fixing the kitchen up.

After four weeks of cracker boxes I had enough left over to buy a $99 futon from the local Meijer's. And a blanket and pillow.

I used a piece of rope to tie my trunk shut with the futon box sticking out the back of it. I bought a 12 pack of Budweiser. Good beer. To celebrate not being homeless no more.

It took me all afternoon to put the futon together with the flimsy Allen wrench they provide. The futon was made in Vietnam and was missing the English instructions. Wonder how much the futon box maker made in Vietnam? I bet his factory hours were pretty heavy, too. With the crude example pictures I got it together, with only three leftover bolts and one lonely locking washer. Spare pieces to cheap furniture is the same in any language.

When I was done with the futon, I was out of beer, and I was hungry. The four hours it took to put the futon together with Vietnamese instructions were the quietest four hours I'd had in months. I needed a radio. My head had a lot of background noise.

I stopped at one of those dollar stores they have on every corner. You know the ones. The dollar stores that sell thirty cent American dreams that are made in China.

I needed an alarm clock. I'd spent the last four weeks with rumbling to life semi trucks waking me up at 4:30am. They had an alarm clock radio for $12 and it shined a laser beam on the ceiling to tell you what time it was. I was on a budget, but it seemed like a steal. I bought some plastic plates and cups, and towels and a dish strainer, and some new socks and underwear, and a few canned goods, and a loaf of bread. It all cost me $33, and I was running out of money.

Bought a six pack of tall boys and a $5 bottle of diesel grade whiskey and two hot dogs off the rotating rack at the corner store. Got a Sunday paper, too.

Ate the hot dogs on the way home to my new crib and only got a little mustard on my beard and none on my shirt or steering wheel. Took that as a good sign.

I set my alarm clock up first thing. Found the classic rock channel on the FM side of the radio. It came in pretty good. They were playing all 80s music.

I put everything away in the wobbly kitchen. All my plastic dishes took up one shelf. Stacked the cans of beans I got for 29 cents in a row. Another row of SpaghettiOs's. The dollar store brand. 59 cents a can. And some cans of sardines. Five cans for a buck is a hard deal to wean yourself off.

I took a long hot shower in the brand new all-one-piece- bathtub and shower stall. It had a little cut out shelf for my new bottle of dollar store brand dandruff shampoo. That set me back a buck. So did my light blue loofah. Exfoliating felt good, though, after once-a-week showers and back seat crick in your neck midnight naps. The hot water lasted 45 minutes. I used all of them.

I sat cross legged on my futon bed listening to 80s rock and eating potato chips. Generic brand. 99 cents.

I spread the Sunday paper out and found the funny pages.

My new apartment was at the back of the house facing an alley. The front of the old house that had been converted into a slumlord investment faced a busy four lane road that went to downtown. Four blocks down the busy four lane road was a giant hospital. Ambulances played siren songs all hours, day and night.

Since the road out front was busy with downtown traffic and wailing ambulances, busy with dope boys circling in lifted Buicks riding on 22-inch tires with shiny spike rims, busy with men from the suburbs, men with good jobs and nice cars, men with nice clothes and bad habits.

Since the road out front was busy, the alleyway was a highway of desperation. Paved over with concrete years ago, and forgotten about since, the alleyway was busted up and broken. I had to drive two miles an hour down it to get to my gravel parking space that was right next to my cracked and crumbling concrete back porch.

The alleyway had no streetlights, so it was dark, and things went on in the dark. The kinds of things they only read about in the suburbs. That's why the men with bad habits have to drive somewhere else to find their vice.

It was getting late on that Sunday night, after my futon building and dollar store- 30 cent shopping spree, and after setting my kitchen up and taking a skin scraping long, hot shower, I was sitting in my new

boxer briefs, on my new futon bed, listening to 80s rock, eating potato chips, and just about to read the Sunday funnies at 10pm when four gunshots went off two houses down the alley from me.

I sipped whiskey and listened to the radio. I read every word of an already growing anemic Sunday newspaper, while a dozen cop cars, and some ambulances, and fire trucks spent four hours cleaning up the war scene. A police helicopter flew around past midnight. Thirty minutes after that, while a half dozen cop cars were still splashing their totalitarian disco lights, a helicopter ambulance flew overhead to the hospital four blocks down the busy front road.

I finally fell asleep around 3 in the morning. My alarm clock radio playing classic rock soft, to block out the all-night traffic out front. And to block out the all-night chatter in my head. The alarm clock radio shined the time on the 12-foot ceiling in foot tall numbers. It said 2:58 the last I remembered.

I woke up the next morning, Monday to a laser hair removal commercial and an ambulance blaring down the street in front.

I found out later that day that a 17-year-old and a 19-year-old were killed two houses down from me that first night in my new apartment.

52.

I spent another week at the cracker factory. Every job in the factory was a temporary job. There were five or eight new people starting every day and different faces packing crackers all the time.

Team leader Tina was in a good mood. Her common law crackhead got a job on a landscaping crew making $9 an hour. He took the family out to Wendy's for dinner.

"Felt good letting him pay for once," Tina said.

Jonesy was Jonesy. He was the same all the time. Laid back, low key, and ready with a joke. Jonesy had found out that I tried to write poetry sometimes, and he was trying out lyrics on me once in a while. Jonesy was pretty good.

On Friday, after our half day of pampering the machines before their weekend off, I went to the corner store and cashed my check and drove downtown to the family court building. It was six stories of brown brick and black glass.

I made it through the metal detector commando squad and waited 45 minutes in line at the family court office. I've yet to find a government office big on urgency or customer service.

When it was my turn at the counter I told the lady my name and told her I needed to change my address.

The government office lady wore circle-shaped John Lennon glasses, a Grateful Dead sweatshirt, and faded blue jeans. She was probably 40 and she had a nice ass. I noticed when she took her piece of paper with my notes on it back to her cubicle to look them up on her computer.

I waited for five minutes. The Grateful Dead government clerk walked over to a printer that yawned for six minutes before printing about 30 pages.

The Dead Head with the nice ass brought the stack of papers over, and she turned out to be pretty chill.

She said, "Your life is a fucking mess" or something like it.

"You missed your mediation hearing. The judge is pissed. Here's your divorce papers. You have a hearing in three weeks on Tuesday at 9:30am," she said.

"Oh yeah," she said. "These last two pages are an arrest warrant for not paying child support. Since its Friday, and you're already fucked every which way to Sunday, I ain't gonna tell the commandos out front like I'm supposed to."

"What the fuck" I said. "I just got child support papers a month ago. How can this be?"

She shrugged. "Have a nice day."

I drove my two-door rusty but trusty Cavalier around the block to a different downtown parking meter. Donated some more hard-earned quarters. Went into a different court. The misdemeanor court. I made it through another group of commando metal detector soldiers. They never suspected I was a wanted man.

I waited 53 minutes in line at the misdemeanor crime clerk's office. Two people before it was my turn one of the clerks went and locked the front door so you could only exit, not enter. When I got up to the counter it was 15 minutes til 5pm closing time.

The clerk that helped me was a middle-aged guy in a polo shirt and khakis. He was the only clerk in sight that wasn't wearing jeans on casual Friday. Khakis were as casual as he could get I guess. He walked like he always had a turd prairie-dogging. His ass cheeks were clenched so tight the skin on his face didn't have any slack to smile with.

I showed him my arrest warrant papers.

"This can't be right," I said. "I just got the papers a few weeks ago. How can I get arrested already?"

"Buddy you don't have time to explain," he said looking at a big circle government clock that looked like it weighed 30 pounds and had been in service 30 years.

"You better give me $150 for bail and let me stamp a court date on here. Go explain it there."

I gave him $150. Got a court date. Walked out of the misdemeanor court with almost half my paycheck gone. Better that than a weekend in jail. And missing a Monday of work at the temporary cracker plant might get me fired. Then what? Back to once-a-week showers that cost $6.

I went to the Salvation Army thrift store on my Saturday off. I found a pretty sweet recliner for $15. And two matching TV trays for $2. A stainless-steel Mr. Coffee coffee pot for $2. A red Teflon coated frying pan with a $18 sticker on it from Target for 25 cents. A pair of carpenter style Levi's, the kind with the hammer loop. There was a small hole in one knee. Size 38x30. 2 bucks. A black Ohio State T shirt, and a blue T shirt that said "I ♥ my Library," on it, both shirts 50 cents apiece. Size XL. I found a copy of *Catskill Eagle*, my favorite Robert B Parker, Spenser novel. Hardcover. One dollar. A paperback copy of the *Tao te Ching*. 25 cents. A paperback copy of *The Color Purple* by Alice Walker. Now a major motion picture, it said on the cover. It won a Pulitzer Prize it said. 25 cents.

I used my worn-down rope to hold my trunk shut over my newfound recliner. I backed my car up to my concrete porch, and my new apartment was feeling more like home.

53.

I went to the HR office at the cracker factory one day at lunch. I told this young pretty HR lady that I needed a Tuesday off to go to court for a divorce hearing.

She told me I had to notify the temporary staffing company. So I went over to their office the next Friday, a week after I had stopped down at the family court.

The round beach ball lady was at the window. She was as round as ever.

I explained I needed a Tuesday off in two weeks.

"Oh, that's a problem," she said.

"Tell me about it," I said.

"The cracker packer factory doesn't like people to miss work," she said.

"Who does?" I said.

I showed her the papers that said I had to go to court. She looked at them. Shook her head slowly. But after 20 minutes of badgering, she told me to make sure I brought in a note signed from court when I was there.

I had left a message with Lorenzo about my new apartment so he could tell Joe, and one evening after work the next week, a week before my divorce hearing, Joe knocked on my back apartment door. He had a 12 pack of cheap beer cans with him.

Joe and I sat on two stolen milk crates I had. We put them out on the back concrete porch, and we sat there with the 12 pack between us and drank beers and watched the traffic walking up and down the back alley.

"You back to work?" I asked him.

"Yes. But fuck that place." He said.

"How's your daughter?" I asked him. I didn't want to but couldn't see any way around it.

"Dying," he said. "She's nine and she's gonna die."

We didn't say anything for the whole time it took to finish our beers, open new ones and drink half of them.

We both looked out towards the alley, people watching.

"You been down at the Bucket much?" Joe broke the quiet.

"Nah. Sometimes on the weekend," I told him.

"Angie asks about you every time I see her," he said.

"What she say?" I asked.

"Just if I saw you. If you're alright and stuff," he said.

We drank some more beer.

"She likes you," Joe said after a while. Joe didn't like it when it was too quiet.

"What's not to like?" I said and Joe snorted, and we both laughed.

A young white girl walked down the alley. She was wearing cut off jean shorts so short that her ass cheeks were hanging out.

Joe whistled at her. She stopped and wiggled her ass at us from the alley. The alley was about 15 feet from my porch.

"How much?" Joe hollered.

"How much you got, Daddy?" She asked from the alley.

"Want a beer?" Joe asked.

"How'm I gone pay my rent with beer?" She asked.

Joe shrugged.

"You lame," she said, and started walking away.

"I come find you later sugar," Joe said.

She laughed and she was gone.

"How you sit here in the evening with all them whores walking by," he said.

"Just like we are now," I said.

We opened new beers and didn't say anything. Three boys around 13 years old bounced a basketball down the alley.

Me and Joe sipped our beers. "You don't believe in God, do you?' Joe said. He was staring out at the alley.

Across the alley from my back porch was another hundred-year-old mansion turned into haphazard apartments, except it had a privacy fence. The house next to it, catty-corner from my porch, had been set on fire and put out. It had wood sheets where the windows should have been and big orange 'Xs' on them to tell you the firefighters said stay out. The grass in the backyard of the charcoal house was about waist high.

An old 30-foot-long white Cadillac with big ass fins crawled down the busted alley. The Cadillac had a good stereo. There were three people in the Cadillac. We all listened to "Many Men" by Fiddy. We listened for about two minutes after they'd drove past.

Me and Joe sipped beer.

"Good stereo," I said.

Joe laughed.

"Does it matter what I believe?" I said.

Joe thought about that.

"Guess not," he said.

Me and Joe sipped our beers.

"Wife thinks God gave my baby cancer cuz I sell drugs." Joe said.

"Fuck, man," I said.

"Yeah. I know," Joe said.

"Then I got to thinking the other night," he said. "While I was wrestling with the fucking machine, what if God really would do something like that? Like, what kind of God would give a little girl cancer?"

I didn't say anything.

"Fuck that God," Joe said.

"I'm with you on that one," I said.

Joe looked at me. I looked at him.

"There ain't no God is there?" He said. "You gotta know. Between you and Lorenzo, you done read every book there is."

"If there is," I said, "I ain't found him yet."

Joe reached over and tapped his beer can against mine and we drained them.

We took our last beers inside my apartment. Joe took a dishrag out of the big side pocket of his cargo shorts. He laid the rag on the TV tray I had set up by my new used recliner.

He took a bent, blackened spoon out from inside the rag and started getting some junk set up and ready to cook.

I'd watched this ritual a thousand times with a dozen junkie lovers and a hundred junkie friends. I'd participated in the ritual a few times over the years. I had to be pretty jacked up to shoot up. I'd rather smoke it. Or crush up and snort some pills.

I'd never seen Joe shoot up before. He took pills like they were candy, and he'd crush and snort like a man that loved the smell of pill dust, but I'd never seen him shoot up.

Joe practiced the ritual of it with enough reverence that I knew this wasn't one of his first times.

I didn't say anything. Just told him "Nah, I don't like shooting it much," when he looked a question at me to see if I wanted to get right, too.

Needles never bothered me. But sharing one gave me the creeps unless I was real fucked up or desperate.

"Wife don't know." He said, and he shot up and nodded out in my recliner. I went and turned the radio part of the alarm clock on. Played country music because I knew that Joe liked it.

Joe left an hour later taking his last beer for the road. His eyes looked empty, and hollow.

I didn't say anything, because me and Joe both knew it, and so did everyone that lived like me and Joe. If you chased the pills long enough, you found the junk. Once you found the junk, you were on a one-way highway to nofucksville, and once you got there, it was next to impossible to go anywhere else. You stayed there until the junk was done with you. I knew it. And Joe knew it. There wasn't nothing to say.

Except that none of my friends that found the junk ever seemed to find God.

54.

I had to go to court again, but this time it was divorce court.

I went through the ritual of showering and dressing for court. I wore my best blue jeans, one of my two button up, church shirts, and my work boots. The boots weren't new, but they weren't bad.

I had a giant stack of legal papers that the clerk at the family court had given me. It had all the papers that my soon to be ex wife's attorney had filed on her behalf, and those papers contained all the things that my soon to be ex-wife and her attorney, were asking for in the divorce.

They wanted full custody. The $150 in child support that they already had going for them, and they wanted supervised visitations for me when I saw my daughters. The attorney had compiled a healthy dossier with records from several of my more colorful adventures with law enforcement.

The big stack of legal papers pointed out that I'd skipped the mediation ceremony and hadn't even bothered to try and reschedule the damned thing. The papers said I'd moved and hadn't bothered to tell anyone. That I hadn't updated my telephone number. The papers said I was a crazed alcoholic, a career criminal, and a doggone menace to society.

On paper it wasn't looking too good for me. Never has looked too good for me walking into government buildings, but I showed up in my good jeans to see how it would go, just like most other times.

The divorce court was a full-on fucking circus. There were so many married people lined up to get divorced that the courtroom couldn't meet the demand. We all had to loiter in the hallway outside of the courtroom until the carnival barker court assistant poked his head out of the big wooden courtroom doors and notified the next three couples at a time that they'd found room for them to sit ringside.

My soon to be ex-wife showed up to the divorce circus with an entourage that took up an entire courthouse hallway bench. Her attorney that didn't like men was there. Her Mom and Dad were there, and her brother, too. It takes a village to raise some kids, and I reckon it takes a village to divorce some others.

The courthouse hallway looked like the stoplights went out at a busy intersection, lots of people in a hurry, trying not to bump into each other, spill their coffee, or make eye contact with any other humans. This was family court, so it wasn't a hallway full of criminals, but divorce court is a popular attraction at all levels of financial and spiritual status, and all those levels were well represented.

There was some guy in a fancy suit juggling two cell phones, and two assistants. He had four attorneys with him.

There was an old couple, lined up and waiting their turn to get divorced. The woman was in a wheelchair and had an oxygen tank. The man was barely getting by with a dollar store cane. They both wore his and her matching gray sweatpants. The old man sat jammed on the end of one of the courthouse benches in the hallway, and every 10 minutes he sniffled and cried a little.

He looked like he was 80. Every 10 minutes the woman in the wheelchair would turn and look at the old man in disgust and say, "Hush, Harold," and she'd stare ice cold killing looks at him that were so fierce that three out of the other four future divorcees of America that were squeezed ass-cheek to ass-cheek on the same bench as poor old Harold flinched every 10 minutes.

There were 2.5 lawyers present for each divorce battle. Lawyers were sipping corporate store coffee and buzzing positive legal affirmations into the ears of their big-spending clients.

After an hour, the courtroom carnival barker called our names and we were in, ringside seats to the great county coliseum. Gladiators and deadbeat dads, prepare to be skewered.

The lawyers were buzzing legal affirmations with twice the intensity the closer their clients got to battle. Family members were lobbing death threat stares like Molotov cocktails with notes in the bottle. All the notes said, "It's your shithead kid to blame here, not our innocent angel," or some shit like that. Shit was tense.

After about three or four divorce wars were settled with lots of blood, snot, tears, wails, pleas and one shout of victory, I got the hang of how things operate in the divorce court coliseum.

Yeah, I'd been married and divorced once, but I hadn't bothered to show up to the divorce court war. I was in another state, conceding defeat on several battlefronts when I received the state sealed decree of my losses.

The Judge that looked like Judge Judy had a tongue 10 times sharper than Judy's. This Judge's tongue was in the same professional league of assassins as Chuck Norris' toughness, Medusa's snake-hair stare, Lil David's giant-slaying slingshot, if the Bible is to be trusted, and the 16-time assassin's cup champion, credit card interest. This Judge had a sharp tongue, and no less than four deputies standing ready to take your cut and bleeding ego to the torture chambers. I didn't know if my heart could take another eight-hour shift of sitting on my hands with my bladder swelling like a fucking water balloon. I decided to play this one polite. Mind my best courtroom etiquette.

About three couples before they called our names to step into the ring, and the whole courtroom stopped. When they called the next fight, the couple called to fight til the other submitted emerged from the galley chaos, and both were wearing dresses. An old man in the back of the divorce coliseum said, "What in hell is going on?" and the whole courtroom broke out in a swell of talking.

The Judge with the sharp tongue brought it all to an immediate halt, and we all stood gawking in silence as the two women made their way to the front. One of the women was transitioning into womanhood and she seemed a little unstable on her heels with all the attention.

I say this with all the judgement I can muster, neither of those ladies deserved this bullshit. No matter what era ignorance lives in, there's no excuse for undressing anyone's struggles. No matter what stage of self-actualization a human is living in, no one deserves to be shamed for fighting to be themselves.

My neck burned red with shame as a sharp-tongued Judge turned tender. This was the only silk pillow fight of all the divorce wars I witnessed that day. Both attorneys and both combatants and the sour turned sweet Judge all whispered their way to a truce that left the jeering, sneering, death glaring, hate staring paid ticket holders in shock until my soon to be ex-wife and I were called to battle.

I'll spare the gory details. There were so many divorces in the divorce coliseum that day that the next day's newspaper didn't have room to cover all the blood and gore. They just listed the box scores. Our box score read that I'd lost big but hadn't gone down without a swing or two.

I walked out of the clerk's office an hour later with papers stamped with the State of Ohio Seal that said I was single again. The papers said I didn't need any supervision to see my own daughters, but I could only see them on Tuesdays from 6-8 pm and every other Saturday from noon- 6pm. The papers said I had to complete 80 hours of how to be a better parent classroom training before I could have my daughters overnight. The papers said that my daughters would have a case manager that would make sure I did all the things single dads were supposed to do to prove they were capable of being dads. The papers said I had to see the case manager once a month for a year. The papers said that I didn't have to have a court supervisor present when I visited my daughters. That was the only point I scored in the fight. The papers said I had to submit to a urine screen once a month when I saw the case manager because maybe I wasn't a full-on menace to society, but there wasn't a lot to say I wasn't, so the papers said I had to jump through 10 times more hoops than the average single Dad.

I walked out of the clerk's office, a single man, a single dad, tired from two lifetimes of marriage and divorce, and two lifetimes of proving my worth, grappling with factory machines. My heart was chewed and half gone from constant civil wars of addiction and trauma. And now I had to mind my best courtroom manners for the next year, just so I could be a dad.

55.

In 2020, 50 percent of marriages ended in a divorce.

60% of second marriages did the same.

56.

After I'd lost big in the divorce coliseum, I went to my back-alley apartment said fuck it and went to bed.

I didn't wake up til 7pm. I woke up as the sun was starting her goodnight routine. Already she'd pulled the drapes on Toledo, and the sky was more gray than not when I woke up confused and disoriented from a six-hour marathon nap.

I took a long piss and scratched my ass on the way to a tired kitchen that groaned when I flipped the light switch. The light was provided by a naked and tired 60-watt lightbulb. A drunk cockroach wobbled across the cracked countertop. I whacked him with a section of leftovers from Sunday's newspaper.

The refrigerator coughed and hacked, and the compressor kicked on. A car went down the alley kicking bass so hard that the kitchen floor vibrated.

I opened the refrigerator. There was a pack of bologna with one piece left in it. I'd failed to seal the package right and the bologna was shriveling from exposure. There was a quarter full, going flat 2-liter of Pepsi, one cup of strawberry yogurt, and a single bottle of Budweiser.

I opened the Bud and drank half. After a six-hour nap it tasted like an oasis.

I went out onto the concrete porch in my boxers. The time was all gray. The halfway mark between evening and night. It was early September. Warm still. I drank my beer looking at the gray.
I could hear gray traffic moving out front on the busy four-lane road. Motorcycles farting their loud farts. The louder the farts the tougher the rider.

Some cars had their mufflers stolen by scrappers, or had their mufflers ripped from their undercarriage by Toledo potholes. Those cars were as loud as the motorcycle farts, but not as tough.

I was hungry, and I needed beer. So I went inside and took a shower. Put clean boxers on. Clean jeans. Work boots. Clean T shirt. Extra spray of smell good.

I got two fast food slime and cheeseburgers for two bucks and a large black coffee for a buck, and I drove over to the Bucket to see Angie.

It was 9pm on a Tuesday night, the slowest night at every dive bar. Only the dedicated, the desperate, and the lonesome get drunk on Tuesday nights.

Bob Seger was singing about "old records" on the jukebox. There were six drinkers around the bar. One couple near the front and four dudes. No one was talking much. Not even the couple.

There was a Tigers game on the TV. Angie was washing mason jars in the sink under the bar. Her tits jiggling in a black Prince T shirt that had a V cut so deep in the front that you could see her purple lace bra peaking out of her bouncing cleavage while she scrubbed.

Someone was sitting in my spot at the end of the bar, back by the pool table. No worries. That happens. I hadn't claimed my spot in two months maybe.

I went and stood down on my end anyway, next to a guy with clean fingernails and a silk polo shirt. The polo shirt was black and had an insurance company's logo on the front.

Angie saw me, her face smiled, and her body jiggled. She came around the bar and kissed me and hugged me. And kissed me again, and that kiss was not the kiss of friends. That kiss had some English on it. Almost had a little French at the end.

"Fuck, you smell delicious," Angie said.

"Fuck, you look delicious," I said, and Angie gave me another kiss. That kiss was wet and warm, and both my heads were on full alert.

Angie went behind the bar and got me a mason jar draft beer and poured us both a shot of Jameson's. She knew Jameson's was my favorite.

The guy sitting on a barstool in my spot, in my home bar, had short hair, a short goatee, and a gold chain that looked like more karats than I could count to.

"Man. I been hitting on her all night," he said.

He lit a Marlboro Light.

"Don't" I said.

He put both hands up in a defeated gesture.

Angie was back from refilling mason jars for drinkers that had nothing to say and no one to say it to.

She introduced me to polo shirt.

"Yeah, I'm in town opening a new insurance office for the company." he said. "Staying over at the Comfort Inn down the road. Nice place."

"Nice to meet you," I probably said.

"My divorce was finalized today." I said, "and I couldn't wait to get off work to celebrate with my new girlfriend."

Angie laughed.

"Niiice." The guy said. "Congratulations."

He bought the bar a round of shots to celebrate. Angie poured me another double of Jameson's on our new friend's dime.

The insurance guy was ok. A testament to not judging a man by his polo shirt. He bought me and Angie drinks all night.

Angie played some music, and we danced.

It was midnight. Two and a half hours til closing time. I had to work in six hours or some shit. But I'd had a half bottle of free Jameson's and a dozen free mason jar beers, and I was feeling alright.

"I was worried about you," Angie was saying, and I was telling her not to.

"Your divorce is really final?" She asked.

I told her it was.

We danced and we got drunk. Angie was kissing me like a woman that hadn't been kissed in a while.

"Tonight's the night?" She asked.

"Seems right," I said.

I helped her stack the chairs up on the tables at closing time so she could run the mop over the floor. She followed me to my back-alley apartment in her car.

The Bucket sold to-go beers for a buck a bottle, so I bought a 12-dollar 12-pack of road beers and Angie stole a bottle of Jameson's. We turned the radio alarm clock on and listened to classic rock and 3am radio commercials.

We sat on my futon and drank, talking a little. Catching up.

I remember Angie taking her clothes off. Her short, thick body coming alive in the light of a dollar store candle.

I remember heat and sweat.

I remember skin smacks, collar bone bites, and growls and groans.

I remember the sun coming up behind the dollar store mini blind.

I remember the back-alley bedroom glowing soft orange, and I don't remember anything else.

57.

I woke up at three in the afternoon the next day. My eyelids felt as heavy as concrete cinder blocks. My eyes were so dry they squeaked when they opened. My mouth tasted like machine dust and muffler rust. My brain hurt like a toothache.

I rolled off the futon and onto the dirty shag carpet. Crawled to the bathroom. Stood up, leaned against the wall, and pissed, mostly in the toilet for 10 minutes.

I limped to the kitchen. Naked. There was a napkin with a note scribbled on it. It was tucked under a quarter full bottle of Jameson's on the cracked and scarred kitchen counter.

I stuck my head under the kitchen faucet and ran cold water over my head until I shivered. Then drank and spit. Drank and spit.

There were two beers left of the road beers. I got one. Found a Tylenol packet with two Tylenols in it. The packet cost a quarter in a vending machine in the cracker packer break room.

I took the Tylenol with the beer. Read the napkin note.

"Couldn't wake you up. I left you a perc on your weed plate. See you soon. XO Angie."

I went in the living room still naked. My weed plate was a paper plate with weed residue ground into it. It sat with my rolling papers on the

TV tray next to my recliner. In the middle of the weed plate was a $10 perc.

Sometimes love sneaks up on us, and I could have almost cried. But I didn't. I sang Johnny Cash songs under a 30-minute shower so hot and thick with steam I couldn't see the gray that lived all around my back-alley apartment.

58.

I was up early the next morning. I made coffee in my thrift store coffee pot. Smoked cigarettes. Listened to classical music turned down low. Read a little from the *Tao te Ching*.

It's a spiritual thing, the way a man spends his morning after fucking up and fucking off for two days. The way one reflects about should haves or should not ofs. The way one measures the amount of fun had against the potential consequences yet to come.

"Fuck it," I thought. If the cracker packer fuckers were gonna fire me, let 'em fire me. Couldn't help having to get divorced, and Angie was fun enough that I thought about her for more than half of my morning of spiritual retreat.

I saw Tina when I got to work. She told me the cracker factory bosses were pissed as fuck at me. Her and Jonesy were telling me that on Tuesday while I was trying to survive death or worse, down at the divorce coliseum no one had told either of the big floor bosses I was gonna be off work.

Guess the whole cracker line stood around for an hour sweeping and taking it easy. Telling jokes and relieved to get a whole minimum wage hour of pay for not having to do nothing but lean on a broom.

They promoted a cracker packer from another line to machine operator. He couldn't figure out the glue build ups and Tina bitched she had to baby sit him.

Jonesy said, "Bro, you fired as fuck."

"Fuck 'em" I said. "I was looking for a job when I found this one."

Sure as shit, about 8am I got called up front to go to the little HR office. When I got up there an HR lady told me I wasn't needed anymore. She said I was to report to the temporary service.

I told her the temp agency told me it was ok to miss because I had divorce court.

"For two days?" She asked.

"Felt like 10. You ever been in the divorce coliseum?" I asked her.

"Who told you it was ok to miss work?" She said.

"The lady shaped like a beach ball," I said.

And that's how I got un-fired. The HR lady laughed until she couldn't breathe. Then she took a drink of water and almost spit it out laughing some more. The next three times she tried to say something to me, she started laughing again.

When she finished with her laughing she told me the beach ball lady was rude to her on the phone all the time.

"And she kind of is shaped like a beach ball," she said.

I was back running my cracker box machine by 8:12am.

At break time, Team Leader Tina said, "Only you could pull that off."

Jonesy said, "I'm glad you didn't get shit-canned. I need a ride home."

59.

Child support caught up with me the same week I got divorced. I went to pick my paycheck up from the temp agency on Friday. My check laughed at me when I took it out of the envelope.

"Good luck living on $250 a week," it said, laughing. Then it kicked me in the balls when I wasn't looking.

I was pissed as fuck. I wanted to kick the shit out of my paycheck, but I knew better than to fight back in front of the beach ball lady.

My paycheck and I talked shit to each other all the way to the corner store where it cost me $5 to cash my check. I bought my weekly carton of Kool's, a case of beer, and a $7 bottle of off-brand whiskey. I walked out of the north end neighborhood carry out with about $180 left to get through seven days of living.

On Tuesday I was supposed to have my first visitation with my daughters. I hadn't seen them in months.

I was supposed to pick the girls up, and their mom was to supposed to get them from my place when the visit was over.

On Tuesday I used the pay phone in the cracker factory break room. I called on every break. No one ever answered except the answering machine and that cost me my quarter each time.

I dropped Jonesy off right after work and headed to go pick up my daughters.

When I got there, my ex-father-in-law told me that I couldn't take my daughters.

I said, "The fuck I can't."

My ex-wife came outside and told me that I didn't have proper car seats for my daughters, so her attorney told her she didn't have to let me take them.

I told her to let me borrow the ones she had. She wouldn't. She said I could just play with the girls in the back yard here at her parent's house. I said not a chance. She said it looked like we had a stalemate.

I said, "I've bought most every car seat the girls have ever had."

I said, "The judge said the girls need both their parents in their lives."

And I said, "You're a no-good cunt, and a special kind of evil bitch."

My Ex-father-in-law called the police on me while I was debating the situation with my second ex-wife. My baby daughters watched out the window as Mom and Dad were taken to separate corners of the yard.

The cops said they couldn't force my second ex-wife to let me see my daughters. The cops said I shouldn't be fighting and arguing and causing a scene in front of my daughters. They said we needed to figure it out, but not here in the front yard.

The cops said I could leave, or they'd give me a ride. I left, smoke coming out of both of my ears, and my battered, bleeding-heart smoldering with hatred and anger.

60.

Every day in the cracker factory blurred into another. It wasn't hard work watching the machine. Easy, really. Half the day I just stood around and watched the machine spit out perfect, bright-colored cracker boxes. On days the machine was on its best behavior, I could have Team Leader Tina keep an eye on it and sneak off for an extra smoke break.

Nah. The work wasn't hard, but the days were impossible. 11 hours a day, standing in an oven. Even as late summer faded into fall the machines and people heated the brick building up, and with no ventilation, it was like standing in an oven for 11 hours a day as sweat drops raced eachother down the wrinkles of your ball sack. Some days I had to change my beard net three or four times.

The days were impossible. Standing with your arms crossed, sweat dripping off chin and ball sack, human desperation growing like a slow-growth cancer. The kind they can't kill with chemo, so you got to live with it for a decade, living a little less each year until the cancer claims your last breath. That kind of slow growth human desperation spreading more each day.

The Cracker Factory let everyone except team leaders wear headphones. Most everyone had these new MP3 players. Little electronic things you could download electronic songs on. I didn't have an MP3 player, and I didn't own any electric songs. I didn't have any headphones.

An MP3 player cost over $100 new, but I could get one for $50 from more than a half dozen of my cracker factory coworkers, but $50 was

$50, and that was a quarter of my weekly check.

I found a little portable radio at a ghetto garage sale that was still open at 6:30 pm on a Wednesday. I paid $2 for it. It was probably from the 70s. I'm not sure. I'm not an antiques expert, just a seasoned thrift store shopper.

The handle was missing so I took the last good boot string out of the left foot of my old work boots. You always keep your old pair of boots as back up in case you have a blow out in the new pair. The boot strings are the first to go. After all these years they still haven't invented a boot string that can match the daily grind of a good American made pair of boots. A good pair of American made boots will last you a year or more. A good boot string about six months.

I took the old boot string and rigged it where the handle should have been and carried my $2 radio into the Cracker Factory. I plugged it into the plug on the side of my cracker box machine. The orange needle that told you the channel you were on, was off by a cunt hair to the right, but the radio that was older than me, worked better than me.

The big boss that didn't speak English looked at me out of the corner of his eye for the first three days. I played the old radio at work, but nobody told me I couldn't have it, so I kept on playing it. I locked it up in Team Leader Tina's desk at the end of every shift.

The old radio made the hours a little better, but the slow growth of human desperation persisted. Even hearing The Rolling Stones twice on two-for Tuesdays on the classic rock station wasn't enough to stunt its slow growth.

The cracker packer that worked closest to my machine was a 35-year-old Mexican woman named Martha. Martha was from Guadalajara, Mexico. She was legal and bilingual. She had the first of three daughters at 15 in a Texas hospital, and they let her stay to take care of her American baby.

Martha had two more daughters by 19 before having her tubes tied. Her husband got deported for the third time a year ago.

She told me she tried to raise her daughters different. She worked hard. Got her G.E.D. Worked two full-time jobs. 40 hours at the Cracker Factory, and 40 hours at an East Side Cantina, where she might have made the best tamales in town depending on who you asked.

But at 35, she had three grandkids, two from her oldest, and one from her youngest, who was 16.

You learn a lot standing less than 10 feet away from someone for 10 hours even if they're dropping a pack of crackers in a box every time the clock's second-hand waved goodbye.

The cracker packer that worked next to Martha was a weird, chubby white dude in his mid-20s. His name was Charlie.

Charlie was a little taller than me, so just under 6 ft, and he was probably 300 pounds. A pudgy looking fella that looked like you could poke a finger into an inch of pudge no matter where you poked into him.

Charlie looked like he took a bath once a week, but he never smelled, except now and again his clothes might have that "left in the washer for two days" sour smell for a week. He just always looked dirty. Had dirt under his nails or something.

He had curly brown hair and blue eyes, and chubby cheeks that his mother probably pinched when she told him how cute he was. No one else never told poor Charlie he was cute though. And his chubby cheeks bounced like Jello when he walked because he kind of stomped with each step. He would have looked mad, stomping around all the time, cheeks jiggling, but Charlie was always smiling the biggest fucking smile all the goddamned time. Charlie was the nicest motherfucker you'd ever meet, and the son-of-a-bitch was immune to the hopelessness all around him.

Charlie was too fucking weird and full of sunshine for me to kick it with, so I was polite but never said much. No one else would have either, except Charlie sold drugs sometimes, and most everyone, whether they spoke English or not, needed to buy drugs from someone, and Charlie had a knack for finding the hard shit most didn't want to fuck with.

"That shit would get a black man a 20-year sentence," Jonesy told me. "But the cops think he's retarded or autistic or some shit, so they don't even suspect him of selling."

"I think it's autistic," I told him.

"Special. Touched. Whatever," Jonesy said, "I ain't fucking with no hard shit."

I never talked to Charlie much, til one day, about a week after I'd been playing my ghetto garage sale radio next to my cracker box machine. It was Two-for-Tuesday and the cracker line had a hiccup. The last cracker packer's cracker hopper had a jammed-up chute and had stopped spitting cracker packages out. Team Leader Tina was getting her ladder on wheels to go over and dive headfirst into the hopper to dig out the cracker package jam. The Rolling Stones came on with "Can't Get No Satisfaction," and with the cracker line taking an unexpected break, Charlie took his headphones off and he could hear my radio playing.

Charlie came over humming the last of "No Satisfaction." It being Two-for-Tuesday, the Stones came back with "Paint it Black," and Charlie sang along word for word.

The radio cut to a commercial after that. The cracker line was still in a brief sabbatical. Both big bosses were headfirst up to their waists in the cracker package hopper with Team Leader Tina.

"That's the best Rock n Roll song of all-time," Charlie said.

"'Paint it Black' is amongst my favorites, too" I said.

And me and Charlie got to be friends, just like that.

61.

I called the family court the day after my ex-wife, my ex-father-in-law and the cops had all refused to let me see my daughters. I used the pay phone in the cracker factory break room.

A clerk told me I was required to have the proper car seats for my daughters. It was the law. She said I could pay $125 to file a motion to ask the judge to force my ex-wife to share her car seats with me. She said the cops probably wouldn't care much about my visitation rights. I wasn't the custodial parent. She said I wasn't allowed to make decisions for my daughters, so the cops would defer to the parent that could.

"That's pretty fucked up," I said.

She said it probably was but if I didn't need anything else now, she had to go, and hung up. Or something like that.

I figured fuck it. I'll buy some thrift store car seats.

Except thrift stores don't sell car seats for kids. The Salvation Army had an entire bench seat from the back of a minivan for sale for $3, but they didn't have a single car seat for baby girls or any booster seats for toddler girls.

Car seats have to be inspected or some shit now. Ever since the auto industry killed some babies with airbags, they started taking child safety in cars serious. By trying to make things safer the auto industry fucked it up for me, and I couldn't find a goddamned used car seat nowhere.

I bought the bench seat from the minivan for $3. Stuck one end in the trunk of my 2-door rusting more everyday Cavalier and tied the trunk down over the other half hanging ass out. It made a good loveseat and came with seatbelts in case the loveseat sitting got bumpy.

It was gonna cost a whole week's pay, after the child support dick kick, to buy two car seats. Shit.

The cracker factory marched cracker package marches. Fall dug in on us, and I didn't see my girls on Halloween. I just worked and drank. Worked and drank.

Angie came over on Wednesdays after I got off work. It was her only weekday night off. We'd order pizza and sit on the futon. The radio played, but we mostly talked and fucked the hell out of each other. It felt therapeutic for both of us. At least I felt better on Thursday mornings. And she said she did too.

I'd stop in and see her once a week at the Bucket. The only time I could afford to go was when Angie was bartending. I'd hang out and if it got dead, I'd try to get her to sneak into the back stock room with me and bend her over a short stack of beer cases. I ain't saying it was love and romance. It was grit and therapy. You either understand, or you don't.

Sometimes I stayed up til she got off and closed the bar with her. We would fuck at my place, then go get coffee and omelets at the all-night Big Boy downtown. We'd chain smoke cigarettes at 4am, chain drink coffee, and talk about how hopeless it seemed for both of us.

The Christian Holy Book says, "The wages of sin are death," and working an 11-hour shift, running a cracker box machine on no sleep felt a little like dying. 10-minute power naps on break time helped a little.

I saw Joe at the Bucket one night when I was up to see Angie. He looked like he hadn't slept in four days and hadn't changed clothes in a week.

Said his daughter was on life support. Said there wasn't any hope for her, or for him.

I said, "Damn Joe. I don't know how the fuck you're gonna get through, but you gotta."

He said, "No I don't. You can't make me."

I said, "I ain't seen my daughters in seven months. That's hard enough. I couldn't make it either, Joe. But you gotta."

We had a couple beers, and Joe left to go home. He was on the day swing of the old machine that I'd flipped off, and even in my slow growing, by the day desperation I still didn't miss that machine.

62.

I went to see Charlie one Saturday. There was an older guy that lived in the front downstairs apartment. He had a fake leg because of a car wreck years ago. The old man would sit on the front porch drinking tall boys all evening.

He got a script for 90 pain pills a month, but he said he only needed 30 of them and he used to sell 60 of them a month to some dude, but that dude got popped and was in jail. The old man had these extra pills and needed money for tall boys.

I gave the old man $3 a piece for his extra pills, and took them over to Charlie, and Charlie gave me $6 a piece for them, and I doubled my weekly pay, and made my rent even if it was a week late.

I went to see Lorenzo but he wasn't at the bookstore. I stopped in at the pawn shop and bought a 10-year-old 19" Color TV set. It had a built in VCR player. I got it for $20 because they'd been making DVDs for nine years and VCR tapes were being phased out.

Lorenzo showed up at the bookstore as I was loading the TV into the back seat of a 2-Door Cavalier, no small feat.

"What dumpster you find that in?" he joked.

He looked like he'd lost 15 pounds in the month I hadn't seen him.

I went into the bookstore with him. He never bothered to turn the "sorry, we're closed sign." We sat in the back room. He passed a bottle of Jack. I passed a joint I'd brought, hidden in my pack of Kool's.

"Lotta people went to jail for this," Lorenzo said.

I asked if he was ok.

"Getting old," he said.

"I heard that happens if we don't die," I said. "Let's stick around and find out."

Lorenzo let me pay for two new books. I bought a book of poems from Dylan Thomas because it had that "don't go gentle into that good night" poem in it. One of my favorites, but I hadn't read too much of Thomas' other poems. And I got a Robert B Parker book. A Spenser novel. My favorite mystery books.

I went back to my back alley apartment. The old man with one leg had basic cable, channels 2-79, and he let me run a cable line through the metal grate that covered his side window in through the metal grate that covered mine, and just like that, I had cable tv.

63.

I found a part-time gig delivering pizzas three evenings a week. With tips, I made about $120 on about 10 hours of work, and in a few weeks, I'd finally bought some brand-new car seats for my daughters. I drove over to the Children's hospital safety inspection and passed with two gold stars. There was no stopping me.

Except baby Mama wouldn't even answer the door when I knocked this time. No one would come to the door. Not my Ex-father-in-law, not my Ex-mother-in-law. Their cars were in the driveway. I knew they were home. I knocked on the front windows. Nothing. Walked around to the back yard. No one was out there. I peeked in the back windows. Nothing.

So I went around to the front, picked up a cinder block they had in their front yard and I smashed it through the windshield of my ex-Father in law's 10-year-old Lincoln Continental. And I split.

The cops knocked on my apartment door two hours later, but I didn't answer. I drank a case of beer and laid on the futon while the TV played thinking of ways to hurt the people that had hurt me.

The next morning, Team Leader Tina told me her husband fell off the crack wagon again. It was day two, and she spent her break time calling all over town looking for him. By day three, she was calling hospitals and jails, driving me and Jonesy nuts bitching about it all.

I went down to family court on another fucking Friday after another morning of polishing the knobs on my cracker box machine. I paid the

$125 to file a court motion so I could get the judge to make my ex-wife let me see my daughters. The family court said that my ex-wife would get a summons to appear to court by certified letter.

I went over to the misdemeanor court. Found out I had a warrant for misdemeanor property damage. I had to pay $150 in bail to stay out of jail. My paycheck was gone. I'd live on pizza tips the rest of the week.

Angie stopped over on Wednesdays. She still didn't know what to do about having a husband that was only her husband on the weekends. I didn't know either, but Angie and I both knew how to fuck, and we both liked to fuck, so we fucked on Wednesdays and talked about her going nowhere marriage, and my going nowhere life.

Team Leader Tina's husband got picked up by the cops for possession and resisting arrest, so he was back home, and Team Leader Tina's life was back to its normal regularly scheduled chaos. She still called him every break, but he was back on the crack wagon, getting the kids to school, and looking for a new job.

I delivered pizzas and didn't mind it. Driving around town, listening to the radio chain-smoking cigarettes while getting paid wasn't too bad.

One evening I went to my back-alley apartment after working in the cracker factory. I had to be at the pizza place in 45 minutes, but I was gonna put my uniform shirt and hat on and smoke a joint before I had to go, and in the middle of smoking the joint my ex-wife knocked on my apartment door. I let her in.

I had the carpet ripped up from the living room and I had dragged it out to the back alley. The living room floor was bare to the ancient wooden floor, and there was a big black mark from the living room bonfire. I had all the kitchen cupboard doors off the cabinets in the kitchen, too, but the slum lord landlord hadn't brought me any new carpet to lay or paint to paint the kitchen and cabinets.

The ex-wife walked in my shit-hole apartment and looked around.

"You really want to bring the kids here?" she asked.

"Fuck you," I said, "What do you want?"

"To talk," she said.

"Can't," I said. "Gotta go to my second job."

"I'll suck your dick," she said.

"Fuck you bitch. Get the fuck out of my house." I told her.

She said some shitty things about my character. I said some shitty things about hers.

She cried. I yelled. She cried. I yelled. And she finally left, and I had to smoke another joint to calm the fuck down.

I was 90 minutes late to the pizza place. The manager was pissed as fuck.

64.

I was broke all the time. Like only enough to buy a cheeseburger, a pack of Kool's and a bottle of Wild Irish Rose every day, broke. The landlord brought some new carpet and knocked some money off my rent for installing it, and I started selling pills and weed. Not like I was a drug dealer or nothing, but in order to keep a little cash flow I sold pills when I could find them.

Angie came over for her regular Wednesday, one Wednesday. It was November. I hadn't seen my girls in a half a year.

It was cold, and the old house that had been carved into apartments had tall ceilings and a cranky boiler in the basement that was controlled by a knob in the front hallway where the stairs were to the upstairs apartments. That's where our mailboxes were, too.

The boiler only worked half the time, so I'd bought a small space heater from one of those dollar stores that are growing like capitalist cancer. You know the ones. The ones that sell American dreams 3 for a dollar. The ones that sell American dreams with high fructose corn syrup.

Angie was over. I had some pills. I'd splurged and bought a bottle of Jack.

Angie told me Joe's kid had died, and the sadness of everything settled over the cold dark bedroom. We drank Jack and watched Jeopardy.

I crushed up the pills, and we took turns ingesting them.

We fucked like every Wednesday, but there wasn't any fun in it. Angie didn't cum, and it took a lot for me to.

We laid in the dark after. Drinking more Jack. The TV playing a sitcom with live laughter.

65.

The cracker factory was grinding my heart and my will to cracker dust. The radio could only help so much. With so many capitalist commercials, the radio has lost a lot of heart and a lot of guts. Add to that, the plastic nature of the music they play on today's radio and the radio could only help so much.

I stopped over to see Charlie after work one night. I'd found some pills, and I knew I could flip half to Charlie for a quick $120, and I could keep a few for personal use and keep a few to sell at $10 a pill.

Charlie lived in a small, old house in Toledo's south end. The house used to be his Ma's house, but his Ma was gone.

Charlie's house was filthy. When you walked in there was a path through the living room with junk and trash piled everywhere. The sofa was clean enough to sit on, and when I got to Charlie's there were two whores sitting on the sofa watching the six o'clock news on a TV with a rabbit ears antenna.

"That's Nikki and my girlfriend Amanda," he said.

"I'm not his girlfriend," one of them said, as me and Charlie went into his kitchen to conduct business.

Charlie's kitchen was covered in pizza boxes, fast food wrappers, empty liquor bottles, beer cans, and drug paraphernalia. The sink dripped a steady stream of water onto a pile of dirty and unidentifiable dishes.

The stove had a four-foot pile of old pizza boxes, empty beer cases, and Chinese take-out coupons.

There was almost a small, clear place at the table, Charlie counted pills there, and gave me my cash.

The kitchen smelled like dirty socks and moldy pizza.

Charlie had a bowl made of aluminum foil.

"Wanna hit?" Charlie said, already holding a lighter under the bowl to get it cooking.

"What is it?" I asked. It wasn't crack.

He used a homemade straw to suck up some smoke. And he held it.

"Heroin" he said inhaling. "I'm scared of needles," Charlie said.

Charlie looked like he hadn't washed his hands in a week. There was dirt under his nails, as he held the lighter under the homemade aluminum foil bowl for me. I took the straw from his fat, dirty hand, and sucked up bitter death. It smelled like burnt vinegar.

I hit the bowl twice. Charlie hit it again. We sat letting the heroin warm our hearts.

Smoking heroin is like getting hugged by a blanket fresh from the dryer and getting your dick sucked by an angel at the same time. Smoking heroin is like hitting a mute button on pain and suffering. Smoking heroin is like taking a deep breath after your head has been underwater for too long.

One of the whores hollered from the other room about us hoarding the drugs.

Charlie smiled. "Oh yeah. The girls. Wanna party?"

We went to the living room. I moved a cat and a bunch of old newspapers off an easy chair that was older than me and sat. Charlie sat between the girls, cut some dope, ground it, and got it lit for the girls.

He cut it, and me and him hit it again. It was the first time I'd taken a deep breath since Joe's kid died.

"Shit. Joe's kid." My brain whispered. Black edges framed all my thinking, and my thoughts rolled by slow and harmless. "I gotta go to Joe's kid's funeral this weekend," I thought, in slow motion.

Charlie laughed. I looked up. He was trying to kiss the whore he says was his girlfriend. She was letting him kiss her.

"Joe's kid" my brain whispered. "Fuck. Fuck. Don't fade out thinking about sad things," I whispered to my heart.

Nikki, the other whore saved me. She came and sat in my lap, and I was zoned, zoned and half gone.

Charlie had his girl laid out on the sofa. Her pants were off, and Charlie's pants were off. His fat, pale-white chubby ass was wobbling around. He knocked over a pile of boxes. One bounced off his back, and he kept going.

Nikki was straddling me, grinding on me in the chair. She was tall, probably 5' 10, and she was skinny with big tits. She had a lot of makeup on.

She took her pants off, and I let her get my dick out of my fly, and I sat there thinking slow. The whore, Nikki was riding me. She was wet and tight on my dick. I could see around the side of her that Charlie had his girl bent over on the sofa now, and he was grunting and fucking.

Slow motion I watched it all happen, realizing too late that I wasn't wearing a condom.

"Oh well," my burned-out heart whispered.

Later, we were out of dope, and Charlie said he had to flip some pills tomorrow at work to get more. Nikki asked if I had a place to stay, and I told her I did. She asked where and I told her. She said she was staying with Charlie and Amanda right now, but it wasn't ideal. She asked if she could stay with me tonight. She said it would be worth my while. I said yes.

213

66.

Nikki rode back to my apartment with me. I stopped and got us some fast-food French fries and milkshakes. Dinner of champions for blue collar junkies.

Nikki took a shower and put on a silk nightgown that barely covered her ass. It was a soft ass. Small, but soft as she spooned with me on the futon. The space heater was cranking on a frosty November night. A shoot 'em up car chase movie played on the USA channel.

Me and Nikki each swallowed a pill from my stash, and drank some Wild Irish Rose, and we fucked again, and it felt good to be drunk and high. It felt good to not feel anything. To not feel the factory aches in my knees and shoulders and hands. To not think about dead kids and kids you haven't seen. To not think about how you're gonna make the rent next week, or whether you were gonna go to jail at next month's court date.

I was between Nikki's legs, hard cock sliding in and out of tight, wet pussy. I laid on top of her, this woman I'd just met, and I pushed into her and it felt so good that nothing else mattered for an hour.

67.

Some say that prostitution is the oldest profession in the world. Upon further research, one finds that dozens of other trades have also laid claim to being the oldest. Doctors, farmers, lawyers, and even tailors, are all trades that claim to come from the earliest days of mankind.

It is known that prostitution as a job dates back at least a few thousand years before Christ was born. The earliest prostitutes worked in sacred temples, and some of those early temples employed male and female sex workers. Crazy, I know, but many of those ancient noblemen of religion and high society, often preferred to fuck men.

There are stories in the Bible about prostitution. My favorite is one about a chick named Tamar. She wasn't really a hooker. She was the widowed daughter-in-law of Judah, one of the 12 sons of Jacob. Tamar disguised herself as a whore in order to seduce Judah, so that her father-in-law could get her pregnant and her offspring could inherit his dad's shit, too.

The Bible has story after story of women using their bodies to influence men.

All around the history of the world's nations, prostitution, or sex work has been a part of who we are as a people. The Greeks and Romans paid to fuck boys and girls, and high-end prostitutes of the day became wealthy celebrities.

In the ancient east, prostitutes serviced farmers, soldiers, sailors, and politicians.

In the Middle Ages there were whores. They lived outside the village or worked on special streets. The Catholics tolerated the prostitutes because paying to fuck was a lesser sin than rape or masturbation.

Protestants came and started to shift the tolerance for sex work, yet it persisted.

Prostitution is part of the founding of our own American history, too. Prevalent in mining towns and urban areas, sex work was actually legalized in St. Louis, and sex workers had to get a license and submit to regular health checks, until the Protestants once again rained on the sex work parade. They protested, and in the United States, right around the time they were trying to get alcohol banned in the 1910s, most states started making prostitution illegal. Blame the Christian temperance movement. They were really hell bent on their husbands not having any fun.

The history of prostitution around blue collar mining camps, is universal all over the world. Wherever a large group of men assembled to do hard work, the prostitutes have also shown up to do their work.

In modern America, paying another adult for the privilege of fucking them, remains illegal in all but a few rural Nevada counties.

Despite being illegal, it is estimated that at any given time there are 1 − 2 million working prostitutes in America.

68.

I had to go to Joe's kid's funeral. I didn't want to go. No one wants to go to a kid's funeral.

The funeral was on a Saturday, and it was at the only funeral home in Joe's tiny Ohio village. I rode the 45 minutes out there with Lorenzo. Tristan was at work at the record store, Saturday afternoon being one of their busy times for selling records.

Lorenzo looked like he'd lost even more weight. His skin was weird and kind of waxy looking. He admitted he'd been tired and just not feeling it lately.

"Watching Joe go through this sure hasn't helped," he said on the way there. We were passing a small bottle of Jack back and forth. A little steel brace to help keep our hearts from collapsing under the weight of the day's sadness.

Joe's whole village and half the rural county showed up to be a part of the funeral. There were so many people wearing their Sunday best on Saturday afternoon, milling around the village funeral home that it took forever to find Joe, but we did, and he was holding up ok with whatever it was he was using as a brace for his heart.

Me and Lorenzo stood in the back of the funeral home as a country Baptist preacher man told us all about God's ways being mysterious. The preacher man told us with certainty that all dead kids go to Heaven to live with Jesus. The preacher man said it was pretty much a big amusement park up there in the clouds, and that Joe's kid was lucky to never again have to suffer the pain of living here on Earth.

After the preacher man was done preaching, everyone got into their cars, and a funeral parade a mile long drove out to a country-side cemetery. The preacher man preached a shorter sermon at the graveside, but it had the same message. It was as quiet as a library as everyone filed by the open grave paying their regards.

There was going to be a big potluck dinner at Joe's family's church, me and Lorenzo skipped out on the casseroles though. I told Joe to get ahold of me later, and Lorenzo asked me if I'd drive back to town.

"Man, I'm just wiped out from all this," he said, and three miles away from the cemetery Lorenzo was napping in the passenger seat.

69.

I got an official letter in the mail that said I hadn't yet registered with the case manager for my daughters. The official letter said that if I didn't come down to their government building and sign up, and talk with a case manager, then I was at risk of losing my visitation rights. I laughed about that.

I had a court date in January for the alleged misdemeanor property damage. The state said I had knowingly thrown a cinder block through a windshield. I laughed about that, too.

I had a court date in family court in February, so I could snitch to the judge about my ex-wife not letting me see my daughters.

But it was the week of Thanksgiving right now, and even the cracker factory shut down for Thanksgiving. It wasn't a paid holiday though, being a temporary worker, working a temporary job. We didn't get any benefits, just a paycheck.

I liked holidays because I didn't have to work, but I never had fuck shit to do on holidays, except drink, and get fucked up. I had a family back in Illinois, I think, but I hadn't talked to them in a few years. They were busy all the time living for Jesus and doing the things that Jesus wanted them to do, and one of the things my family knew for sure was that Jesus did not want them to have much to do with a drunk, divorced drug addict that didn't believe in Jesus.

Nikki was hanging around some when she didn't have any customers, and I still didn't know her last name, but when she was over, she had taken to straightening up the apartment, and that was kind of nice.

I asked her what she was doing for Thanksgiving, and she told me she was going to her mom and dad's. She had a five-year-old son that they were raising and she liked to go see him on the holidays.

I found out that Lorenzo was going to hang out with Tristan's parents for the holiday. Tristan's parents were about the same age as Lorenzo, but they weren't too judgey about who Tristan loved.

I'd quit delivering pizzas and just sold pills and weed to supplement my income, so I was home after work on Tuesday before Thanksgiving, drinking a beer with Nikki, and asking her how her day had been. Nikki was telling me that she had an old guy customer that was in his late 60s, and he couldn't get it up anymore because he had high blood pressure, but he liked to lay his head in Nikki's lap and have her rub his hair.

Joe knocked on my back-alley door. I let him in, and he was in bad shape. He was pale white, and sweating, and looked like he had been sweating in the November cold in the same clothes for a week.

Joe was looking for pills or dope, and I had some pills that I was going to sell, but I gave Joe two of them, because he was my friend and he needed them, and Joe had always shared his pills with me when he had them.

Me and Joe and Nikki all took pills, and I asked Joe what he was up to. He didn't say, but he hung around a while, and then he took off. Said he might stop up at the Bucket late in the evening on Thanksgiving to see me and everyone else.

When Joe left, Nikki and I went to bed on the futon, and watched TV. Nikki spooned against me and I took her pants off, and forgot all about Joe, and how bad he looked. I forgot about everything for a good 30 minutes.

70.

I stayed up late closing down the Bucket on a rowdy Thanksgiving Eve. I was fucked up drunk and blasted on pills, and Angie had come back with me to my shit-hole apartment after the Bucket closed, and we'd listened to music, and got more drunk and fucked til the sun came up, and Angie had to get back home. Her husband was coming in around noon and Angie was going to her in-laws for Thanksgiving dinner. I wished her luck when she left, and I finally passed out around 7 in the morning, so that I woke up late in the afternoon that Thanksgiving, with a headache and a bladder full of last night's bad decisions.

I went down to the Bucket to celebrate the holiday. It was six in the evening, and the Bucket was celebrating in the common neighborhood dive bar tradition. All the regulars with nowhere else to go were hanging out, having a potluck thanksgiving.

There was a ham and a turkey, but the turkey was spent after being picked over by lonely drunks since noon. There were store bought pumpkin pies, cookies, some kind of green bean casserole that looked sketchy, and of course there was football on the TV like every Thanksgiving.

I said hi to some of the regulars, and got some Ham, some store-bought deviled eggs, and a piece of store-bought pumpkin pie with a healthy dollop of cool whip. Happy fucking Thanksgiving to me.

I drank for about two hours, and then Joe showed up, and Joe was looking just as rough as he was two days before when he'd stopped over at my place.

Joe was looking for pills or some dope.

I wasn't out of pills, but I told Joe that I was. I bought him a drink. Tried to ask him how he was holding up.

"I gotta go. Gotta find some junk," he said. "It's the only thing that makes the hurt go away."

"I know, Joe, but you know that shit don't work forever." I said and bought him another drink.

"Nothing else comes close," said Joe, and he stayed for one more round, and he split to go find the things that took the hurt away.

I left about 10, went home and got drunk on cheap wine and late-night television. Happy fucking Thanksgiving I thought as I fell asleep alone in a big cold bedroom.

71.

Thanksgiving was just a temporary reprieve for the temporary workers at the forever cracker factory. We were all back on Monday, and Monday was the same as every Monday. The box machine jammed up every 40 minutes. The break bell rang every two hours. Cracker dust chipped away at the soft parts of our hearts.

72.

As long as there has been prostitution, there's been the question of how and why one would choose to be a prostitute. In some ancient societies, the children followed the parent into sex work. Yes. Not just girls and women. Some studies estimate that at any given moment, 20% of the working prostitutes in the world are male.

How and why does one enter sex work?

The holy prostitutes, working the holy temples, were often born into families of holy prostitutes. But in some cultures, humans were captured, enslaved, and human trafficked into the work.

Whether the sex workers are working in a holy temple, selling their bodies for the pleasure of god, or working outside a run-down mining camp or outside of a big conservative convention in Nashville, they may, or may not, have willingly become whores.

Some people become prostitutes against their will. Some people become prostitutes because of a lack of good paying jobs in their area.

Some people become prostitutes because they're abused as children. In fact, almost every sex worker study says that almost every sex worker has sex before their 14th birthday. That's the one great indicator, universal amongst all studies: sex workers are almost always exposed to sex at a young age.

We could spend the rest of the day debating the thousands of studies about the how and why of people choosing to be prostitutes, and we would never come to any one set of conclusions.

In the end, does it matter the how and why? Or does it only matter if the sex worker is willingly employed?

I've known my share of prostitutes. I've dated two working whores, and I've paid a dozen others, in various ways, for the pleasure of their bodies. Some of those women had pimps. Some of them might not have exactly chosen to do the work they were doing.

I have done things in life that have hurt others, and I have had hurts done to me. None of that serves as an excuse.

There have been many instances of successful, regulated prostitution, all throughout history. Likewise, there have been just as many that have not been favorable to the sex worker. It must be noted somewhere, and if not in the official annals of scholarly lore, then let the record show it's said here: every study in history shows that religion has seriously screwed up sex work.

Let it be said, too, for the record, that Jesus Christ himself befriended prostitutes, and eunuchs. I read it for myself, straight out of a cheap motel's Gideon Bible.

73.

The cracker factory was there every morning, before the sun came up. It was there when the sun went down, and there when the sun was all around. I'd been massaging and un-jamming the same cracker box machine for six months, on a temporary basis. I got a 50-cent raise, still no benefits. I was making $10.50 an hour now in my temporary, permanent, full-time job.

It was between Thanksgiving and Christmas, and Santa Claus wasn't coming to this part of town. There wasn't any holiday cheer in a back-alley apartment in the north end of Toledo.

Nikki was hanging out part-time. Angie was hanging out on Wednesdays, and I was hanging on by a thread, twisting in the December wind.

The weekend after Thanksgiving, I went to see Lorenzo because I didn't have anything else productive to do. Lorenzo was not at the bookstore. No one was. I could see Doc the cat napping on a big box of books by the counter, but no one was home.

The weeks between Thanksgiving and Christmas are some hard fucking weeks to get by. In a world of bullshit, there's extra bullshit to get through during the holidays.

First, the liquor stores are busy as fuck. It's like first of the month every day in December. People getting together with their families and loved ones need extra liquor to get through it.

Second, everyone is fake cheerful. Everyone says Merry Christmas or Happy Holidays, depending on which side of the social civil war you're on.

Third, traffic is a bitch, and everyone is stressed the fuck out, and no one seems to be cheerful. People are ringing bells everywhere, and every charity in town is asking for your change.

Fourth, more people go to the neighborhood dive bar. More people at your daily home bar is never a good thing.

Fifth, Christmas music.

Sunday I stayed home. I had a case of cheap beer and a bottle of cheap wine. I put the alarm clock radio on the country music channel because it seemed appropriate. I decided to finally paint the kitchen so I could save some money on rent.

I lined up all the cabinet doors on some newspaper on the counter and I cracked a can of paint. I was a third of the way done with the front of the first door, and I'd heard my fourth Christmas song already.

I switched to a local pop hip hop channel.

I was jamming, four doors deep when Joe rattled the glass in my back door.

Joe was full-time on the junk. He didn't try to hide it. We were both too close to the junk all the time for him to try.

He asked if I had pills. I said I did but they cost money and that I didn't want to sell him any.

Joe got pissed.

"Fuck you. You know Lorenzo's got cancer?" He said.

Joe had stopped at the bookstore earlier in the week. Tristan was there, too.

"Lorenzo looks like he lost 40 pounds. Tall as he is, he's bones, man," Joe said.

"Fuck. Fuck. Fuck." I said.

It was pancreatic cancer, Joe told me. Stage four.

"Tristan had to help him stand up," Joe said.

Me and Joe did some pills that Sunday. We drank a case of beer. Drank a bottle of wine.

My heart hurt, and it was tired. I didn't know how much more my heart could take. But it was good to kick it with Joe. Just like old times.

74.

I didn't set an alarm on Monday, so I slept til 10. Kind of on purpose. I got up, and drank half coffee half whiskey for an hour, then ate a pop tart.

I showered and went over to the bookstore. Tristan was there with another young guy, a friend of his.

He said Lorenzo was at the hospital again. Said he didn't want visitors. Said he might get out by the weekend.

"I know we don't believe in god, but pray," Tristan said.

I went to the Bucket, and got drunk hanging out with Angie, went home late, fucked up and hungry and pissed off at the world.

Nikki was at my apartment when I got there at midnight.

"Where you been?" She said.

"Bitch who the fuck are you to ask?" I said.

She was sorry. It didn't matter. I told her to get the fuck out. And she did.

I woke up three hours later in the morning, still a little drunk and still pissed off.

The cracker factory gave me a hard time for missing Monday, and I told them to get fucked. Three weeks before Christmas, I quit my job.

230

75.

I spiraled for days. I got hammered drunk and did some pills. Then I traded some pills for some coke, and I mixed coke and pills with whiskey. I hadn't done coke in a minute, and you shouldn't do coke and pills and whiskey together, but I did, and I got spun out for five days.

There was a crazy bitch that moved upstairs above me. I'm not being mean. Hell, I've laid out a detailed list of my own crazy. But this bitch upstairs was crazy, and she set my new living room carpet on fire trying to make meth using a car battery she stole from down the block.

I'd ran into her in the alley. I was walking back three blocks from trading three OxyContins for about $40 in crack. She was walking back with a Rite Aid bag and a car battery. She'd boosted some cold medicine, and I don't know how the fuck it was supposed to work, but I had a bowling ball sized black spot in the middle of my new carpet.

Her name was Traci. She had big tits and wore combat boots. She was thinking about shaving her head in protest of not having custody of her four kids.

I told her I couldn't see my daughters either, and I was protesting too. She went upstairs to get clippers and I locked her out. My carpet was still smoldering.

Traci shaved her head on my crumbling-concrete back-alley porch. She took her shirt off, stood topless, and shaved her head with rechargeable clippers.

I let her in after she was done. I had the carpet fully put out and I threw the car battery in the back yard. There was acid leaking from it.

I wouldn't shave my head, and Traci got pissed, and said I wasn't a real revolutionary. She was though. She let me watch as she shaved her pussy with a mirror and straight razor. Told you the bitch was crazy.

It was a wild week.

76.

A week after I quit my job, I slept for a day and a half, recovering from being up and fucked up most of the week before. I was back down again, and Team Leader Tina stopped over at my apartment with Jonesy. I was glad to see them. They said I could probably come back to work because the cracker packer factory needed someone to run my cracker box machine.

For two days more I said, "Fuck that place," but then on the third day, a week and half after I quit I went back to the cracker factory. They tried to take my six month raise away, but I bitched and they let me keep it.

10 days before Christmas and I was back, un-jamming the glue sprayer on my cracker box machine and running the cracker line with my old teammates.

The cracker factory didn't care I was there, or not. They made just as many cracker boxes as always.

Lorenzo was back out of the hospital two weekends later, but I had to go see him at his house. It was the first time I'd ever been there. He lived in a big old house in the old West End of Toledo. His house used to be a mansion, and still was, if you didn't mind a hundred-year-old mansion.

Lorenzo was sitting in a library room in his antique mansion. He looked like he'd been battling with death every night the last three weeks since I'd seen him.

"What up old timer?" I said.

We smoked a joint together.

"Lotta people went to jail for this," I said, when he didn't.

They had him on a methadone pump for pain, and his eyes were glassy.

We talked for an hour about our favorite books. We agreed that *East of Eden* and *The Color Purple* were in the top five, but Lorenzo picked *Slaughterhouse Five* over *Still Life with Woodpecker.*

A week before Christmas, and me and Lorenzo never even acknowledged the holiday.

77.

Old man Christmas finally showed his ass. It was 10 degrees and gray with no snow and the boiler that was 100 years old gave up its ghost and died.

It was cold as fuck with frost coating the inside of the windows. It was Christmas Day and all the stores were closed except for the 7-11 and the Rite Aid down the road. I went to the Rite Aid and bought a second small space heater for $30.

I put a blanket over the doorway in the big bedroom and with two space heaters it started warming up, but the water was frozen in some pipes somewhere in the house.

Traci upstairs, and my bedroom were on the same fuse in the ancient fuse box, and the fuse blew. We couldn't find any more fuses, so I said fuck this shit, and me and Nikki, who was done hanging out at her parent's house with her kid, went to a dive bar across town and got drunk on liquid holiday cheer, and then we went and stayed the night at a motel that charged $24.99 a night.

It was warm and toasty in the motel, and me and Nikki exchanged presents even though we hadn't bought each other anything.

78.

I had to work a few days between Christmas and New Year's, and none of the holidays they did give us off were paid holidays, but what the fuck was I gonna do? Get pissed and tell them to get fucked again? And fuck myself over more?

I tried calling my ex-wife from the cracker factory break room pay phone because I'd bought the girls a couple of things for Christmas. I might not have given two shits about your Christmas cheer, but that wasn't the girls' fault.

My ex must have been overcome with Holiday cheer, because she answered and didn't hang up on me.

"What if I bring the girls over on New Year's Day," she said, and I almost fell.

The landlord had come through with a new furnace for the old house, but he paid these two crackhead handymen to put it in on the cheap and it took them four days, so we lived without water for four days but the space heaters kept the bedroom warm. The furnace sounded like a shotgun going off in the basement every time it fired up.

Then, on New Year's Eve afternoon, me and Joe were supposed to go see Lorenzo. When we got there, Lorenzo was gone. He'd went back in the hospital two nights before, and Lorenzo died on the morning of New Year's Eve.

Instead of visiting with Lorenzo, we got to try to console Tristan. Me and Joe didn't do a very good job. We weren't much suited for consoling ourselves.

It didn't seem fair that a kind man like Lorenzo would find love and companionship and die in less than a year, but I knew Lorenzo knew life wasn't fair.

I tried telling Tristan that Lorenzo left lucky. He left loved by Tristan and by me and Joe, and many others. Tristan cried harder when I told him.

Joe was besides himself. He'd already suffered too much loss in recent weeks.

"I'm going to get right," Joe said.

"I can get some pills," I said.

"Don't need 'em," Joe said.

Joe had a rig under the front seat of his pickup truck, and he was preparing to use it, right in the front seat of his truck in front of Lorenzo's.

I left him there because I'm selfish and because my friend Lorenzo was gone, and I didn't know anyone else that knew how exciting it was to find a new James Baldwin book that you hadn't yet discovered. Who else would understand that I liked the way an old book smelled almost as much as I loved drugs and pussy. No one else, but Lorenzo had understood.

79.

My ex-wife brought my girls over the day after Lorenzo died. It was New Year's Day. A new year. A new day. Same me living the same crazy life.

My ex-wife parked her mother's minivan in the frozen dirt patch next to my rusting more by the hour, two-door cavalier. I helped her get them out of the van. They were both walking, and the factory machine had robbed me of watching one take her first steps, and chaos and addiction had robbed me of a do-over.

Both my daughters were wearing red and white Christmas dresses, white faux fur coats, and even in the hard frozen dirt of a back-alley north end yard, they looked like little waddling angels.

By bringing the girls over, my ex-wife had meant she was coming over with my girls. I didn't give a shit. There wasn't an in-law to call the police on this holiday party.

I made chicken nuggets in the oven and I read the girls their new books I'd bought them for Christmas. One was a Curious George book, and one was the *Giving Tree* by Shel Silverstein, but my ex-wife said that was too sad to read to a toddler. I said it was a beautiful love story. And she said it taught you to use those you love. As usual, we didn't see eye to eye on what love meant.

My youngest daughter shit her pants and it leaked out of the top of the back of her diaper and on her tights and dress. My oldest daughter started crying and the furnace kicked on like a fucking shotgun blast, and the house shook. I needed a fucking drink, and the ex-wife got pissed at me for cracking a beer in front of the girls.

"It's one beer," I said.

"Yeah but the divorce papers say you're not supposed to drink," she said.

"The divorce papers say a lot of things you don't give a shit about," I said and she started putting the girl's coats on.

"I thought for a moment that we missed you," she said.

"I thought for a moment you weren't a cunt," I said.

She stormed out with the girls and they only took half their Christmas presents I'd gotten them.

New Year's Day. It was shaping up to be a long fucking year.

80.

Nikki didn't come around for two weeks and Joe moved in. Lorenzo's funeral was a perfect gray January funeral with fat snowflakes falling at the cemetery and a salt truck leading the funeral procession back to a Unitarian church. Lorenzo's parents were 80-something and refused to attend the Unitarian potluck dinner. Tristan got drunk on sparkling champagne and had to be helped to his parent's car by 8pm. Joe was nodding out in a corner as the funeral director was shooing us, and a smorgasbord of multi-gendered and grieving humans out the church doors.

81.

I found out Nikki was staying away because her ex was out of jail.
Fuck it. You win some you lose some. I had other shit going on.

Joe had gotten kicked out of his house because he'd quit going to work,
and his six-year-old daughter told her mother she saw daddy giving
himself a shot one night when she couldn't sleep.

Joe wasn't working. He was crashing on the minivan bench seat in my
living room and only leaving for a few hours a day to hustle dope, pills
and wine. Joe would leave at sunup and drive around the hood in his
pickup looking for scrap metal. He only needed $50 a day to get right
and get by.

I was grinding away in cracker boxes. I had a court date coming for
misdemeanor property damage, and one Friday afternoon when I'd
just gotten home with a case of beer and a double order of hot wings,
a case manager from family court showed up with two cops. The case
manager wanted to inspect my apartment and make contact with me to
see why I hadn't been to see her.

Joe kept falling asleep sitting up on the minivan seat, and there were
empty beer cans laying around, a few of which Joe had sawed in half
with a pocketknife and used to cook crushed up pills on.

The case manager told me it was a violation of my court order for
visitation to be in a home with alcohol and drug use present, and after
a lot of questions and note taking the cops left me alone, and Joe fell
back asleep while I ate my cold hot wings.

82.

One day halfway through the first month of a new year Nikki stopped over one evening. Joe was nodding out on the minivan seat, about to crash without an airbag.

Nikki said her ex-boyfriend was back in jail. I said I didn't care who was in jail.

She said she didn't have a place to stay other than Charlie's again. I told her I didn't care who lived with Charlie.

She asked could she stay tonight. I told her my dick hadn't been sucked for three days.

It's not that I was all dead-heart, steel dick. I didn't give a fuck Nikki stayed the night at a trick's. She got paid extra for that. Business is business. But if she was giving pussy away to someone else, that was different to me.

Didn't matter too much though, because just like that, Nikki was back hanging out.

My heart was cold and fading, but my futon bed smiled for an hour that night.

83.

The cracker factory fired me and Charlie two days before my misdemeanor court date.

Me and Charlie had weekends free from the cracker factory, and the women we did weekend things with were busy on weekends. Charlie was a genius junkie. He knew more ways to get fucked up than anyone I'd ever met.

Charlie's Mom was a crack whore. There's no reason to tell it different. Charlie spent his childhood in a crack house with a crack whore mother, and he stayed til she died an old woman at 41. And now his childhood crack house was his house.

Me and Charlie kicked it one Saturday with this Mexican American girl from the cracker factory. She was 19, born in East Toledo and liked to get fucked up and bought drugs from Charlie all the time.

She'd come over to party and Charlie told her if she hung out topless she could party for free. She had great softball-sized tits. Mocha skin and small copper nipples that rose like a tiny fist when you flicked them. I did flick them. The Mexican American 19-year-old girl was naked in 15 minutes and playing with herself. I'd given Charlie $30 and we somehow had $150 worth of crack and heroin. Sweat and vinegar smoke filled our lungs and our hearts and filled Charlie's dirty kitchen like a desperate opium den.

The ole South End crack house rose again, and it don't get near the respect the devil gets in New Orleans but let this stand testament that a 19-year-old beautiful junkie girl made me feel like the devil had earned his due here. More than one boy was ruined here.

A mouse ran from under the stove and lost itself in a pile of garbage that hid all but the open lid of an ancient garbage can.

The crack and heroin had my heart racing and my brain crawling in slow motion. The strain was too hard for my Bi-Polar heart, and I said "Hey Charlie. Go easy on our girl here. I gotta split."

"Don't you want to stay and fuck me?" The girl said.

I did. But my heart wouldn't let my brain say it that I wasn't going to fuck her after Charlie's fat ass played around with her. I just turned around and left.

I got fired on Monday morning because that 19-year-old girl overdosed on Sunday afternoon. She was ok, but still in the hospital.

I didn't even argue about it. As I was leaving Charlie was trying to catch up. "Bro, we started shooting Sunday morning. She kept wanting to do more," he said.

"Fuck you, Charlie. Fuck you," I said. My heart was sick and my brain was dry heaving. How did a 19-year-old with an angel body get that close to hell?

No one has written a ballad to a South End Toledo crack house. The devil dances in Toledo cemeteries, and Toledo junior highs just the same. The devil dances on Broadway, on both sides of town. The devil left New Orleans and his wreckage has devastated the Midwest worse than Vietnam ever dreamed of doing.

There's ballads about the ruin of a whole generation of pill mill babies, but the devil gets his respect, whether the piper pipes, or writes.

I went home and shot up with Joe. We got right for two days before I remembered I was supposed to be in misdemeanor court.

84.

I was a day late to court. There would be a warrant out for my arrest. I had family court coming up, and I was unsteady about how that was going to go.

I'd just got fired from a temporary job I didn't want, and I was falling further behind on my child support. In the first month of a new year I didn't know how much more of this old life my heart could take.

I had $37 so I bought a case a beer, two packs of smokes, and bottle of Andy Capp hot fries for 99 cents. I bought a Toledo newspaper that was a shadow of its old self.

I drank beer and listened to the radio. Tried to think about what to do next. I hadn't stopped and thought about much in a while, and there was a lot to think about.

The alarm clock radio played the local top 40 pop station that was leaning towards pop hip hop. After too many Kia car commercials, I switched to the pop country station that was leaning towards pop tractor hop. They sang about belt buckles and pickup trucks in the corn fields. There was still a lot of dirt roads on the country channel, but they sounded different than when Johnny Cash drove them.

I read the newspaper that needed a blood transfusion. It said George Bush was losing a couple of wars and that gas prices were on the rise. It said the NFL playoffs were almost over. It said there was going to be a Super Bowl, and that commercial prices were sagging from last year. A 30 second ad cost a measly $2.3 million, the near 10% decrease in the value of the Super Bowl dollar was a sign a recession was coming.

I read the newspaper that was two months now on the kidney transplant list. It said the economy was bad. It said factories were bleeding jobs because the American worker didn't have enough money to buy enough things. It said factories were being left abandoned like capitalist ghost towns, because it was better for Wall Street if there were more factories in Mexico. And China.

The newspaper with jaundice said that you could build factories for pennies on the capitalist dollar in China.

The newspaper with type 2 diabetes so bad that it was on the verge of having 5 out of 7 daily print issues amputated, said that you could pay Chinese factory workers peanuts and rice for their family back home, and that was 30 cents an hour compared to an average American manufacturing wage of $20 an hour.

The newspaper with melanoma in its heart said, "Good luck finding a decent job."

The help wanted ads barely wanted any help. There was an ad for a door-to-door vacuum salesperson. There was one for a warehouse mattress salesperson. There was one for a part time flower delivery van driver. 20 hours a week. $8.50 an hour. And one as that said, "Steel Workers Wanted. Must have steel toed boots and be able to pass a tape measure test. $11 an hour. No background checks." And it listed a temporary company on a shinier side of town.

I'd found the needle in no haystack. I drank another beer to celebrate.

Joe came home when I was a dozen beers deep and a half dozen hours of thinking and figuring in.

Joe was fixing his rig on a plastic porch chair I'd found in the alley one day. It was one of those $5 summer specials from the corner dollar store. The back was limp, so we had to leave it propped in the corner, but you could still see the TV from there.

"Joe," I said. "I got to get my life together."

"Sure," Joe said, balancing a spoon and trying to draw a syringe from it one handed. He was doing a pretty careful, good job.

"Joe," I said. "I found another job, I think. You want to go with me tomorrow to see?"

"Sure," Joe said. He was inserting a needle in his wrist. There was a rubber string around his forearm.

I didn't have any heart left to keep at it. I'd thought about it for six hours. All I knew to do was to get up tomorrow morning, take a good hot shower. Put my good blue jeans on. Lace up my steel toed boots again. And go see about offering whatever heart I had left, to a steel plant.

85.

When Ronald Reagan was elected President in 1980, there were nearly 20,000,000 American factory jobs. Since 1980, his first year in office, America has lost nearly 8,000,000 factory jobs. Half of those factory jobs now live in China.

86.

Before I could shower, and apply at the steel plant, Joe OD'ed the next morning. He didn't go into a coma or nothing. He didn't die. He just went unconscious, and he was breathing weird, like his lungs were trying to get rid of all the air in them, and that was making him foam at the mouth a little.

I dragged him to the shower, and it took what seemed like 10 minutes to get him there. Joe weighed about 275 pounds. I turned the cold water on. Water was spraying everywhere, and Joe moaned and coughed and coughed and started puking a little.

It took us about 10 minutes but Joe came around.

I got drunk that day and watched TV with my friend Joe. We ordered pizza, and we both got drunk, and stayed away from the junk.

Nikki came over late. She'd had a bad day. Two tricks today in different zip codes around town. Lots of bus transfers, and all-day busses were running late. Nikki took a long shower and put on a black Ramone's T shirt of mine. Her hair was still wet, and with no makeup she looked almost 23 again.

The furnace kicked on with a shotgun blast as Nikki curled up next to me on the futon. David Letterman was on the TV, when Joe said, "I'll leave you two be. Wake me up tomorrow. Let's go see about that job," and Joe left the bedroom.

The space heater was cranking, and Nikki showed me she wasn't wearing anything under her XL T shirt nightgown, and it was almost warm in my back-alley bedroom for the first time in months.

💀

Special Thanks

A thousand thank yous to Michele McDannold the kick ass editor of Roadside Press for always believing in my work. We wouldn't be holding this book in our hands without her tireless work. Thank you, Michele. I owe you forever.

Thanks to artist Richard Modiano for his indispensable help in editing this book, and for all of his warm thoughts and well wishes. It's been an honor to work with you, Richard.

Thanks to writer A.S. Coomer, a longtime collaborator and close friend, for writing a foreword so beautiful I almost wondered if he'd read a different book by mistake, except he quoted some great lines from the work in his foreword, just like the professional writers do. Thanks buddy. Love you.

And thanks to artist Patrick McGee, another longtime artist friend and creative inspiration that has taught me so much about being a working artist. Thanks for the amazing cover to this book, Patrick and for all your friendship and support over the years.

Thanks to my children: Spenser, Iris & Cheshire for putting up with Dad's shenanigans all the time. You three are and forever the lights of my life. Hope you never meet half the characters I knew in this novel.

And thanks to John Zidarin, to whom this book is dedicated, who when I was 90 days sober in 2006, asked "what do you want to do in life?" And when I replied "be a writer," told me to start writing. When I replied "how?" his answer, "I don't know. But if you want to, you'll find a way," changed my life forever. That and for teaching me that a life free of my addictions was the only path to true freedom. He died in 2016, but I'll love him forever.

252

Dan Denton is a former UAW chief steward, and union autoworker. He is a veteran of four dozen different factory jobs and is currently a full time writer. His work has often been featured in magazines, union journals, and newspapers, and has been widely published amongst today's best underground and independent artists. He is the author of the novel *$100-A-Week Motel* (Punk Hostage Press, 2021) the poetry/novella hybrid *Finding Jesus & Prayers To My Saints* (Gutter Snob Books, 2022) and several chapbooks of poetry. He has lived and written in Toledo, OH for the last 20 years.

MORE ROADSIDE PRESS TITLES:

By Plane, Train or Coincidence
Michele McDannold

Prying
Jack Micheline, Charles Bukowski and Catfish McDaris

Wolf Whistles Behind the Dumpster
Dan Provost

Busking Blues: Recollections of a Chicago Street Musician and Squatter
Westley Heine

Unknowable Things
Kerry Trautman

How to Play House
Heather Dorn

Kiss the Heathens
Ryan Quinn Flanagan

St. James Infirmary
Steven Meloan

Street Corner Spirits
Westley Heine

A Room Above a Convenience Store
William Taylor Jr.

Resurrection Song
George Wallace

Nothing and Too Much to Talk About
Nancy Patrice Davenport

Bar Guide for the Seriously Deranged
Alan Catlin

Born on Good Friday
Nathan Graziano

Under Normal Conditions
Karl Koweski

MORE ROADSIDE PRESS TITLES:

The Dead and the Desperate
Dan Denton

Clown Gravy
Misti Rainwater-Lites

Walking Away
Michael D. Grover

All in a Pretty Little Row
Dan Provost

These Are the People in Your Neighbourhood
Jordan Trethewey

They Said I Wasn't College Material
Scot Young

Radio Water
Francine Witte

And Blackberries Grew Wild
Susan Mickelberry

Licorice Heart
Miles Budimir

Disposable Darlings
Todd Cirillo

Full Moon Midnight
Belinda Subraman

Innocent Postcards
John Pietaro

Cistern Latitudes
James Duncan

Another Saturday Night in Jukebox Hell
Alan Catlin

MORE ROADSIDE PRESS TITLES:

Abandoned By All Things
Karl Koweski

Ain't These Sorrows Sweet?
Lauren Scharhag

She Throws Herself Forward to Stop the Fall
Dave Newman

We Don't Get to Write the Ending
Aleathia Drehmer

These Many Cold Winters of the Heart
Ryan Quinn Flanagan

Things You Never Knew Existed
Josh Olsen

Green Roses Bloom for Icarus
Hiromi Yoshida

Let the Scaffolds Fall
Shaun Rouser

Apocalypsing
Jason Anderson